Chandrakanta

For Nilanjan
& Abhimanyu.

Best-wishes

Shashi Deshpande

Chandrakanta

DEVAKINANDAN KHATRI

Translated and retold by Deepa Agarwal

Introduction by Prasoon Joshi

PUFFIN

PUFFIN BOOKS
Published by the Penguin Group
Penguin Books India Pvt. Ltd, 11 Community Centre, Panchsheel Park, New Delhi 110 017, India
Penguin Group (USA) Inc., 375 Hudson Street, New York, New York 10014, USA
Penguin Group (Canada), 90 Eglinton Avenue East, Suite 700, Toronto, Ontario, M4P 2Y3, Canada (a division of Pearson Penguin Canada Inc.)
Penguin Books Ltd, 80 Strand, London WC2R 0RL, England
Penguin Ireland, 25 St Stephen's Green, Dublin 2, Ireland (a division of Penguin Books Ltd)
Penguin Group (Australia), 250 Camberwell Road, Camberwell, Victoria 3124, Australia (a division of Pearson Australia Group Pty Ltd)
Penguin Group (NZ), 67 Apollo Drive, Rosedale, North Shore 0632, New Zealand (a division of Pearson New Zealand Ltd)
Penguin Group (South Africa) (Pty) Ltd, 24 Sturdee Avenue, Rosebank, Johannesburg 2196, South Africa

Penguin Books Ltd, Registered Offices: 80 Strand, London WC2R 0RL, England

First published in Puffin by Penguin Books India 2008
Copyright © Deepa Agarwal 2008

10 9 8 7 6 5 4 3 2 1

ISBN 9780143330417

Typeset in Minion by Mantra Virtual Services, New Delhi
Printed at Pauls Press, New Delhi

Contents

Introduction

In a somewhat rickety jam-packed state government bus heaving down a winding road from Almora to Haldwani en route to Delhi, sat a bony twelve-year-old bespectacled boy crammed near a window seat, holding tight a shaking book with both hands, eyes burning into the bouncing text. This is what I remember so vividly of my first mesmerizing encounter with Babu Devakinandan Khatri's *Chandrakanta* and his *mahajaal*.

A restless traveller with awkwardly long legs, I used to hate sitting cramped up and eagerly looked forward to any stop where I could get off, stretch my legs, sample a roadside snack and explore the surrounding area. But during that particular journey, I sat inside the bus mindless of the stops. In fact a kind of a rhythm had been established between the movement of the bus and the world of the tilism; a static bus was a break in that rhythm. It was a fantasy so gripping and fascinating that when I looked around I started to imagine an aiyaar in my fellow passengers. An encounter with reality was not desirable: it jarred compared to the world Babu Devakinandan Khatri had invented.

Later, I was to realize that I wasn't the only one entrapped in the world of Chandrakanta and Virendra's love story that played out against a backdrop of warring kingdoms, with mysterious and endearing characters like Chapla and Tej Singh, the vile Krur Singh and Shivdutt, and my favourite aiyaars and aiyaaras. Generations of young and old alike had been ensnared by the magic of this tale and have distinct memories of when they first read *Chandrakanta* and its sequel *Chandrakanta Santati*. They remember borrowing the book from an uncle to while away time on a train journey and reading it through the night in dim light; or escaping to the *chatt* (roof) of the house to continue reading uninterrupted; of hiding the book from an overzealous father who thought it wasn't a subject fit for children; of coming across the book in a library and begging for it to be issued; of tenth standard grades suffering due to the obsession with reading all the volumes of the book; of being surrounded by grown men who could not read Hindi and being begged for the story to be read aloud to them.

Chandrakanta is a swashbuckling adventure, with warring armies, sword-fights, treason, deception, gallantry against magical creatures and in dire situations. With their omnipresent bag of tricks the aiyaars—specialists in warfare and spy work, masters of disguise and magical powers—could impersonate any person, or sometimes even an animal, often with the noble intention of furthering his king's cause. Woven into this tale is a tilism—a kind of maze containing many secret passages, traps and prisons—which has to be 'broken', or deciphered by a chosen person. The person who successfully breaks the tilism gains the immense treasures hidden within it.

The land is described in detail and you can picture the area, as well as the mood, vividly. The battlefields, dark caverns, forests or the beautiful secret prison where the aiyaars keep their prisoners safe, are places that one can never forget. The secret prison with its hills, waterfalls, gentle breeze rustling the jamun trees, the peacocks dancing are so wonderfully depicted that you feel you are really present there. The characters are described and developed in detail, be it the beautiful Chandrakanta and Bankanya or the 'dakini' Surajmukhi.

It's a documented fact that this book by Devakinandan Khatri made a strong contribution to the learning of the Hindi language by the people of the times.

In the ancient period of Hindi or Adi kaal (before AD 1400), Hindi literature developed in the northern states of Kannuaj, Delhi, Ajmer and adjoining areas. It was during this period that the famous *Prithviraj Raso* was written by Chand Bardai, considered one of the earliest works in the history of Hindi literature.

The Bhakti Movement left its influence on medieval Hindi literature and long poems and epics were composed during this time. Avadhi and Braj were widely used dialects. A priceless classic from this era is Tuslidas's *Ramcharitmanans*. This was also the age of tremendous integration between Hindu and Islamic elements in the arts.

During the late 1800s *khadiboli* developed amongst educated Hindus. *Khadiboli* was heavily sanskritized. It was also called Sahityik Hindi (literary Hindi). To distinguish themselves from the general masses, learned Muslims now wrote in Urdu which borrowed from Persian and Arabic vocabulary. Soon Urdu became the dominant language of the classes and much of the masses alike.

It was in this milieu that Devakinandan Khatri wrote *Chandrakanta*. It is considered to be the first authentic work of prose in Hindi in the Adhunik kaal (modern period). This book brought the Hindi language alive and into the limelight although many terms are of Urdu origin. People were so eager to know what happened next, they started to learn Hindi just to be able to read the works. The author wrote 'bayans', or chapters, and these were published and distributed widely. People would enthusiastically await the new bayans which, legend has it, were auctioned hot off the press.

It wasn't that Hindustani culture had a dearth of fiction. Storytelling is a part of our ethnicity and has a rich tradition. And whilst words are important everywhere, in India the spoken word has always played a pivotal role. Our country has an enviable oral culture. Stories and fantasy tales have been recited through generations. Folk tales and even epics have been passed from one generation to another without the use of written words. Recitation and listening, in forms like *katha vachan*, are still alive in India.

But while many stories are contextual, only a few transcend boundaries and find place in the minds and hearts of generations to come. There is something about *Chandrakanta* that remains suspended in time.

But what was it apart from the writing that captured the minds of readers? There was no social statement; no revolutionary thought. Was it pure entertainment?

I think much of *Chandrakanta*'s popularity also had to

do with our belief in miracles. Do miracles have any place in our modern, scientific lives? Consider this: while surfing television channels mid afternoon or late night, have you paused at teleshopping programmes selling products you would never find anywhere else? It's called interactive home shopping. Through the programme innovative appliances usually not available in traditional outlets are sold. That's what the marketing definition would, I presume, say. Delve a little deeper and various other versions come up.

Let's look at the products they sell: A steam tent that you can sit comfortably under and lose weight; except that it looks like you are being swallowed by some alien entity. Machines, belts which are plugged around your waist, working away 'those muscles' while you go about doing your regular (in)activity. Lotions that promise to make you fairer or taller; an apparatus that will make naturally wavy hair poker straight; a wonder drug for diabetes . . . The list of these tasteless products is endless.

Or go to a mela and take a look at the amazing exhibits: a magic potato peeler that can undress a dozen potatoes in less than half the time; a duster that will dust every crevice of the impossible to clean cassette racks; haldi stain removing liquid; a wonderful soda maker promising 'cold drinks' at home. Even the most prudent buyer in us cannot help but stop and watch for a while before flicking channels. Our logic questions the products but I have known many to have punched that number and ordered a cream, a belt, a powder, all in the hope that it will produce the miracle we so hope for.

My belief is these products play on our wish for magic. There is an underlying, rarely acknowledged thought within many of us that there maybe something out there which is being kept hidden away. If we find it, we will get what we desire. Have we not at one time or the other wished for a time machine, hoped to discover something as miraculous as Aladdin's lamp, imagined a hidden treasure in the ancestral home, dreamed that in the snake hole in the tree trunk there could be a *paras mani*, or that if we followed the rainbow to its other end there just might be that pot of gold.

So when you read about the amazing qualities of the stone flowers that Virendra and Tej Singh discover in the tilism— of the rose flower that acts like a knock-out drug or the oruhar's paste that ensures hunger doesn't strike for four days or how the exhaustion of a thousand-mile journey vanishes when the traveller's feet are washed in the paste of the oleander flower—a chord is struck.

If the world was only about logic and reality then there wouldn't have been emotions, relationships, exceptional sacrifices, heroic deeds and passion. Pandit Omakarnath Thakur, a renowned Hindustani classical vocal artist, wanted to sit in a lion's cage and sing, confident that no harm would come his way, such was his belief in the power of his music, his art.

Ordinary facts from our everyday life—that we can fly to our destination, or we can talk to people thousands of miles away through a small instrument—all started with a dream and a belief in what seems to be miraculous.

I am personally a huge admirer of Darwin's revolutionary work. His theory of evolution and natural selection should have destroyed belief in God or a higher power—especially in the West. But it was not for weakness in the logic of Darwinian theory but the poetry in the concept of God, that billions have kept their faith alive. Your mind may question the existence of God but your heart accepts it fully. *Chandrakanta* reintroduces us to that side of our being that wants to believe in wonders.

Devakinandan Khatri was a colourful personality. He was a warm-hearted gregarious man who loved exploring ruins of old forts and ancient structures near his hometown and areas where he worked. The strange tunnels and surprising trap doors that he discovered in the forests of Chunar kindled his interest in mystery writing.

He wrote *Chandrakanta* and much of *Chandrakanata Santati* sitting on a *takth*, or a marble platform in Sri Har Mandir in Bihar. There are some who claim that his inspiration was *Dastaan-e-Amir Hamza*, a Persian work written earlier and performed by Dastangos all over Delhi and north India in the early part of the twentieth century. But I would like to believe that such a large volume of work could be produced only by an original thinker. Only a truly great writer could have created so enthralling an epic-romance with such variety of scene and character, such ingenious largess in creation and portrayal with so much pace and humour in the narrative that readers irrespective of age are left as eager as wide-eyed children for what's going to happen next.

Chandrakanta Santati is a much more monumental and complex work than *Chandrakanta*, spread over six thick books. It is the story of the sons of Virendra Singh and Chandrakanta, and has the added attraction of a mysterious aiyaar called Bhootnath, who has a magical dagger. Bhootnath played such an important role in the book that there followed a separate book on him, called *Bhootnath* which in fact ran into seven volumes. Devakinandan Khatri also wrote many other works including *Kajar ki Kothari* and *Gupta Godana*. His son, Durgaprasad Khatri, had a pivotal role to play in the development of the later works but no one can doubt the storytelling prowess of Devakinandan Khatri.

I still remember sitting in the Zilla Pustkalay of a small district of Rampur. My father was a district level officer and had the jurisdiction of the library as well. But he was unaware that using his clout I would get the library opened up at odd hours in the afternoon or late evenings. It's here that I discovered a treasure trove of books and with my appetite already whetted by *Chandrakanta*, read more books on *jaadu* and tilism. It was sometime before I could lay my hands on *Chandrakanta Santati*. I devoured whatever I could find of that genre of literature in that library. Many a times I have thought of making that journey back to Rampur if only to ensure that this rare form of writing is preserved for many more years; that the surreal world it depicts continues to exist in the minds of those fortunate enough to have come by it, as it does in mine.

I was indeed fortunate to have read *Chandrakanta* in Hindi when I was a child and I congratulate Puffin for unearthing this gem and bringing it alive for this generation. For whilst children and adults are enthralled by *The Chronicles of Narnia* and Harry Potter, to be introduced to the kind of world an Indian writer had brought alive nearly hundred years ago is amazing.

When you read this book you will understand the power of writing and the beauty of narrative. There's a delicious immortal magic in this work.

Read the book and you will know that a tilism can be cast only by an accomplished person. It is an enchanted zone which is both a physical reality as well as an imaginative effect. It seems that Babu Devakinandan was a sorcerer in disguise for he created in *Chandrakanta* such an enchantment that it has a magical effect. So fasten your seatbelts and get ready to embark upon a journey that will take you into a world you will never want to leave.

Jai Maya.

August 2008   Prasoon Joshi

Chandrakanta

The Lovelorn Prince

The day was fading and just a few traces of sunlight remained. The Vindhya mountains stood out darkly against the luminous sky. Two young men sat on a flat rock in a deserted meadow beneath a low hill, deep in conversation.

The taller, Virendra Singh, dressed in a brocade coat and silk turban, seemed to be of royal birth. He was, indeed, the only son of Maharaja Surendra Singh of Naugarh. The other, Tej Singh, who was the same age—twenty-one or twenty-two—was the son of the dewan or prime minister of the kingdom, Jeet Singh. Virendra's closest friend, he looked restless and kept glancing around. A dagger hung from his trim waist and a large bag was slung on his left shoulder, while he impatiently flicked the rope he held in his hand. A horse, saddled and ready, was tied to a tree close by.

'Tej,' Virendra said, plucking bits of grass from the ground and flinging them down again, 'there's nothing more miserable than to fall in love!' His large eyes were dark with gloom and his well-shaped lips drooped beneath his moustache. 'You've been carrying my letters to Chandrakanta, brought hers back for me to sigh over. We adore each other. Our kingdoms are barely ten miles apart. And yet we're doomed to separation.' He examined the piece of paper in his hand. 'See—again she's written, "We must meet, somehow".'

'We could set off for Vijaygarh this very minute,' Tej Singh said, his supple fingers caressing his dagger. 'But Maharaja Jai Singh, her father, has surrounded the palace with soldiers. It's impossible to get in. Worse, the prime minister's son, Krur Singh, has taken a fancy to Chandrakanta as well. Knowing she cares only for you, he's charged two aiyaars Nazim Ali and Ahmed Khan to watch her constantly.'

'They can't possibly be cleverer than you at the art of disguise and trickery!' Virendra frowned.

'Certainly not!' Tej twirled his moustache proudly. 'I have tricks in this bag that no one can match. But I don't want to smuggle you in without getting rid of them. That idiot Krur Singh—*he* dares to dream of marrying the princess! He's instigated Jai Singh to double the guard.'

'Tej!' Virendra clutched Tej's wrist. 'I *have* to meet Chandrakanta. I can't live without her. I'm afraid . . . she might think I'm a coward or don't care enough.'

'It's too risky, my friend,' Tej shook his head. 'But don't worry. I'll leave for Vijaygarh right away and try to get to her. Her companion, Chapla, who is utterly devoted to her, is an accomplished aiyaara too. She will be a great help. However, we must find out our enemy's plans.'

The prince gazed at the letter and bit his lip savagely. 'But Chandrakanta must be waiting for me!'

'And what if the guards catch you and throw you into the dungeons? How will you meet her then? Let me spy out the land first.'

Their eyes locked for a moment. Then Virendra sighed. 'All right,' he said reluctantly. 'I'm relying on you. You have to find a way. I must meet Chandrakanta. But go now.'

Tej jumped up and set off on foot. Virendra untied his horse, mounted it and rode off towards his fort, which was visible at a distance.

*

Little did Virendra and Tej know, but that very moment, Krur Singh was conferring with his aiyaars, Nazim and Ahmed.

Krur paced up and down his opulently furnished baithak. Lean, with a hawk-like nose and close set eyes, he tugged at his sparse moustache as he schemed against the prince. Nazim and Ahmed listened, reclining comfortably against satin bolsters.

'This is a sorry state of affairs, Nazim,' Krur's voice rasped with indignation. 'The maharaja doesn't think I'm good enough to be his son-in-law. Chandrakanta is besotted with that fool, Virendra. Even if I carry her off by force, my purpose will not be served.'

Both men nodded. Krur continued, 'We should capture Virendra and his aiyaar Tej Singh and confine them in a place so remote that no one can trace them for a thousand years. Then I can worry about putting his majesty out of the way, grabbing his throne and enjoying life with Chandrakanta. What say you, fellows? But will the people of Vijaygarh accept me as their ruler?'

'Don't you worry about that,' Nazim's thin mouth twisted in a crooked smile. 'We'll organize support. But you have to promise us the most important positions in the kingdom— that of your chief ministers.'

'That goes without saying,' Krur replied promptly.

'But . . . uh . . . we'd like it in writing,' Ahmed's narrow eyes were cautious.

'You will have it at once.' Krur Singh's eyes flashed.

Nazim promptly produced some paper and a pen. Krur Singh quickly wrote down what they dictated, signed and put his seal on it.

The two aiyaars rose, all smiles. 'And now we'll go and see what our lady is up to,' Ahmed smirked. 'It's the pleasant hour of evening. No doubt she'll be strolling in her garden— sharing her tale of woe with her companion Chapla. It won't be hard to find out what's up between her and her lover.'

Krur guffawed loudly and slapped Ahmed on his back. 'Good luck,' he said.

The two left, salaaming deeply.

Hullabaloo in Chandrakanta's Garden

There was still a glimmer of light in the garden where Chandrakanta was taking the air with her companions Chapla and Champa. A faint breeze stirred the evening air, carrying the scent of flowers—juhi, bela, motia and roses. The departing rays of the sun glanced off the mango trees on the west of the garden, lighting them up. The freshly watered flowerbeds were a splash of brilliant colour against the green of the clean, washed trees. The high walls of the palace and its turrets, silhouetted against the evening glow, made a dramatic backdrop.

Chandrakanta's dearest friend Chapla, living up to her name, flitted about busily, plucking flowers and bringing them for Chandrakanta to admire. But the princess's delicate features were drawn and her normally sparkling eyes had deep shadows under them. Her friends had dragged her out into the garden but nothing seemed to lighten her gloom.

Distressed, the gentle-faced Champa wandered off into a thicket of malti bushes to pick a bouquet to divert Chandrakanta. The princess drifted towards the fountain in the middle of the garden and gazed listlessly at the water spiralling out.

'Where's Champa?' Chapla asked, coming up behind her.

'She must be around,' Chandrakanta shrugged.

'I haven't seen her for quite a while,' Chapla frowned.

'There she is,' Chandrakanta said indifferently.

'Why is she walking in that peculiar way?' Chapla stared at the approaching girl.

Champa ran up to them. 'Aren't they beautiful?' she said, presenting a bunch of flowers to Chandrakanta. 'If Prince Virendra Singh had been here, he would surely have rewarded me for my artistry.'

The princess's face immediately turned wan. Tears poured out of her eyes. 'God knows what fate holds for me,' she said, her voice barely audible. 'What sins did I commit in my previous birth that I have to suffer like this? I can't understand what's taken hold of my father! Despite Virendra's pleas, he says he'd rather I remained unmarried. That wretch Krur's father Kupath Singh has him in his clutches. The fool Krur actually wants me to marry him!'

Chapla squeezed the princess's hand hard and frowned at her. The princess looked puzzled, then went silent, suppressing her sighs. She strolled ahead, still holding Chapla's hand. After a while, Chandrakanta threw a quick glance at her friend and deliberately dropped her silken handkerchief. When they had gone some distance, she stopped, pretended to search, then shrugged.

'Champa!' she said. 'Could you see if I dropped my handkerchief near the fountain?'

Champa hurried off obediently. The princess turned to Chapla, 'Why did you signal that I stop speaking?' she whispered.

Chapla cast a guarded look at Champa's receding back. 'This person isn't talking or behaving like our friend,' she said. 'I'm getting suspicious.'

She cut her words short. Champa was returning with the handkerchief.

Chapla turned to her as if she had just remembered something. 'Did you do what I asked you to last night?'

'Uh-h, I forgot,' Champa replied.

'Do you even remember what it was?'

'Oh, look, there's a spider in your hair,' Champa reached out, quickly changing the topic.

'Oh!' Chapla brushed her hair with a cursory hand. Then she stuck a finger in her ear and wiggled it. 'Oh-h! I think it's crawled into my ear!' she cried. 'Can you take a look?'

Champa grasped her elbow and propelled her to a better lighted spot. She peered into Chapla's ear.

Chandrakanta, who had turned to snigger into her handkerchief, started when she heard Chapla call, 'Come quickly, my friend. Look what's happened to Champa!'

Champa was sprawled on the ground, oblivious to the world. 'I stuffed a tiny pouch containing a special powder in my ear,' Chapla said grimly. 'The moment she smelt it—' She shrugged meaningfully.

'I hope you haven't wronged our Champa,' Chandrakanta frowned.

'I'm quite sure I haven't,' Chapla said. She hoisted Champa on her back and lugged her to the fountain. The two splashed water on her face and scrubbed it hard.

And Champa's face transformed itself into Nazim's!

Chandrakanta turned red with rage. But Chapla said, 'Just see how I settle this smart fellow.'

She dragged the man to a cellar that lay beneath one of the turrets in a corner of the garden. Being an aiyaara, Chapla possessed considerable strength and could carry even a full-grown man with ease. As the princess watched, she took out a candle from her equipment bag and lit it, illuminating the room. Swiftly, she bound Nazim's hand and feet. Then she held smelling salts to his nose. The aiyaar sneezed and opened his eyes.

Nazim's face grew ashen when he realized what had happened. Then Chapla picked up a whip from a corner of the room and cracked it menacingly, and he paled further.

'Forgive me! I'll never do it again!' he cried.

'Why did you come here? Tell me at once. And what have you done with Champa?' She cracked the whip again.

'I-I sprinkled a bouquet with knock-out drops and threw

it in her path.' Nazim's teeth were beginning to chatter now. 'She picked it up, sniffed it and fainted. Then I dragged her into the malti bushes and put on her clothes . . . Let me go now! I've told you everything.'

'Not so quick, my friend!' Chapla said. She turned to Chandrakanta. 'Will you watch him while I look for Champa?'

The princess nodded. Chapla found Champa lying unconscious among the flower bushes, as Nazim had said.

'And how are you, my gullible friend?' she asked, when she had revived Champa. 'Got nicely taken in, didn't you?'

'How was I to know someone was up to tricks around here? Where are my clothes? That was an expensive outfit,' Champa said sulkily.

'Here!' Chapla tossed her some of Nazim's discarded clothes. 'You'll have to make do with these.' Reluctantly Champa put them on.

Then Chapla took her to the cellar where Nazim lay imprisoned. 'You can thank this gentleman for your state,' she said.

Furious, Champa began to beat Nazim, who cursed Krur Singh for his fate. The three girls then left Nazim there and returned to the palace.

Tej in Action

'Wonderful!' Tej Singh said to himself, as he stood in the shadows, gazing at the walls of the Vijaygarh palace. 'It's even more heavily guarded than I thought. If it had been a dark night, I could have thrown a rope over and climbed in unobserved. Well . . . '

He prowled around for a while. Then he found a lonely spot, disguised himself as a macebearer and made for the main entrance. Some officers sat there, along with a few soldiers.

Tej approached one. 'Isn't the moonlight superb, sahib?' he said. 'I've been in his majesty's service for just four months and being off duty, came out to enjoy it. I got a whiff of your tobacco and was overcome by a craving.'

'You're welcome to try it. Come, have a puff, my friend.' The officer extended his hookah.

Tej took a couple of draws, then began to cough loudly. 'This is strong stuff, my friend. Too strong for me. Wait a bit, I think I have some of the maharaja's own brand. His hookah bearer is my friend and gave me some. Would you like to try it?'

'Why not?' said the man. 'You are a lucky fellow, I must say.'

Tej produced some tobacco and the officer eagerly filled his hookah, which began to gurgle merrily. It was passed around, accompanied with much jolly talk. Slowly, the loud chatter faded to a whisper, as the soldiers grew dizzy and slumped to the ground. Soon they were sound asleep.

At once Tej Singh darted through the gate and entered the garden. His eye fell on a maid carrying a light. He lassoed her with expert ease. She fell like a struck tree. Before she could utter a cry, Tej placed the knock-out powder beneath her nose. He dragged the unconscious girl into a corner, hurriedly put on her clothes and made himself up to look like her. Then he entered the palace and headed for the room where Chandrakanta was sitting and chatting with a group of her maids. Chapla and Champa were there too. He sat down quietly in a corner.

'Why, Ketaki,' Chapla said immediately, 'I'd sent you on an errand. Have you completed it that you're sitting there so silently?'

Tej Singh replied in a woman's voice, 'Well, I did set out to do it when something strange caught my eye. I came back to tell you about it.'

'Oh! And what was that, may I ask?' Chapla said.

'Ask these girls to leave. It is meant only for yours and the princess's ears,' the fake Ketaki replied.

When all the maids had gone, Ketaki laughed and said, 'First promise me a handsome reward for the news I've brought.'

News of Virendra, was the first thought that flashed through Chandrakanta's mind. But Ketaki was not supposed to know anything about the prince. 'Of course I'll reward you,' she said. 'But tell me what it is first.'

'No, you must give me my reward first,' was the demand.

This infuriated Chapla. 'What's wrong with you today? How have you become so bold? I'll fix you, if you don't behave.'

'Do you think you're stronger than me?' Tej Singh, dressed as Ketaki, said mockingly.

Chapla sprang on her and grabbed her hair. But as the two were grappling, Chapla suddenly realized that she was fighting with a man. Immediately she drew her dagger and said, 'Tell me who you are right away, or you're done for!'

Tej Singh simply stepped aside and placed Virendra's letter in front of Chandrakanta. The moment Chapla's eye fell on it, she guessed who Ketaki was. She flushed with embarrassment, though in her heart of hearts she couldn't help admiring Tej's cunning.

Chandrakanta quickly read the letter, then asked, 'Tell me Tej, is he all right?'

'How can he be all right, your highness? He refuses to eat or sleep, just sighs and weeps over your letters. He was insisting on coming along but I forced him to stay back. Said I'd check out if it was safe for him, first.'

'Oh, how I wish you had brought him! I'm longing to see him! If only my father would listen to me. This wretched Krur Singh has poisoned his mind against Virendra. But I have something to tell him too, now that my dear friend Chapla has captured Krur's aiyaar Nazim.'

She narrated the incident and Tej Singh was astonished to learn that Chapla was so accomplished. As he gazed at her admiringly, his heart pounded with a stronger emotion.

But after a while, he said, 'Chapla has been very smart indeed. However, she has slipped up a bit.'

Chapla frowned. 'What do you mean?'

'Didn't you guess that if Nazim was there in the garden, Ahmed must have accompanied him too? Why did you leave Nazim unguarded in the cellar?' Tej replied. 'You should have confined him in the palace or presented him before the king right away. Ahmed must have set him free by now.'

Chapla paled. 'You're right,' she said sheepishly. 'I did make a big mistake—but it didn't occur to anyone till now.'

'Why would it? You call yourself an aiyaara, believe you're sharp-witted; aren't you expected to consider all the possibilities? Well, let's go and see if he's still there.'

Chapla dashed to the garden. When she reached the cellar

she found the door wide open. Hoping against hope she hurried down the stairs. The room was empty!

She returned to the palace, cursing her foolishness. 'What am I to do?' she said. 'Ahmed *has* set Nazim free.'

Tej Singh smirked. 'So you considered yourself a great aiyaara,' he taunted. 'You claimed you were quick and clever and possessed all sorts of great qualities. And a very ordinary aiyaar put your nose out of joint!'

Chapla flared up. 'If I don't grab both and produce them right here, I'll change my name!' she said vehemently.

'Indeed! I've witnessed your expertise,' Tej grinned. 'Now watch how I catch them and imprison them in my own city.'

Tej then told them how he had entered the garden and described the spot where he had left Ketaki unconscious. 'I'm not going to return her clothes,' he said. 'I plan to leave in this disguise. Don't let anyone get the slightest inkling, or my plans will be ruined.'

'All right,' Chandrakanta said. 'But Tej, you must come here every two-three days. It's a great comfort for me.'

'Just as you wish,' Tej bowed.

But as he prepared to leave, the princess broke down. 'Oh Tej, am I not fated to ever meet the prince?' she wept.

'Please control yourself,' Tej said gently. 'We're working to make that possible. If you give up hope, how will we carry on?'

Chandrakanta wiped her eyes and tried to smile. Tej bowed and left. When he reached the palace gate he found some of the guards still asleep, others trying to shake off their stupor. A couple had returned to their senses.

'Are you supposed to guard the gates or hug the ground?' he scolded them. 'Why do you take so much opium? You can't even keep your eyes open. A dead man would be more alert. I'm going to report you to her majesty, the queen.'

The guards who were awake froze with fear. 'Please, Ketaki,' they folded their hands. 'It was one of those wretched macebearers! He offered us such poisonous tobacco that it knocked us out totally. That fellow was trying to finish us off! He fooled us this time, but if it ever happens again, you're welcome to do whatever you wish.'

'All right, I'll not report you this time. But don't you dare do it again!'

Tej flounced off. The guards were so terrified that they did not dare to ask Ketaki where she was going at that hour.

*

Hidden in a tree, Ahmed had seen Chapla capturing Nazim. He observed the princess returning to the palace with Chapla and Champa, and that Nazim was not with them. Convinced that they had imprisoned him somewhere in the garden, he began to search. When he neared the cellar in which Nazim was confined, he heard his shouts. He quickly opened the door and untied his friend. 'Hurry, let's get out of here,' he said. 'Then tell me what happened.'

Once they left the garden, Nazim told him how Chapla had penetrated his disguise and beaten him up.

'We have to act fast,' Ahmed said. 'This Chapla is becoming too smart for our good. Worse, she's training Champa too. Together, the two will give us a hard time. We have to capture Chapla and put her out of the way.'

'First thing tomorrow,' Nazim said. 'It's too late today. We'll put her away in a place so remote that no one will ever find her.'

The two walked along, plotting and scheming. When they reached the other gate of the palace, they noticed Ketaki approaching them.

Tej Singh recognized them at once. It was too good an opportunity to miss—he could capture at least one of them, if not both. He deliberately went past them, to arouse their curiosity. Sure enough Nazim and Ahmed began to follow him.

After a while, he turned and said with a frown, 'Why are you following me? Go and take care of your own duties!'

'What do *you* know about our duties?' Ahmed grinned.

'I know everything. Go, get another beating from Chapla! What can you accomplish? You don't have a single helper there—not even a maid.'

The girl's cunning struck Nazim and Ahmed dumb.

Finally Nazim found his voice. 'Listen, Ketaki,' he said, 'our job is to outwit others. If we worry about getting caught and beaten up, we can never achieve anything. A few clever words can fetch us thousands of rupees. And sometimes by God's grace, we find accomplices like you. If you help us, we'll give you a share.'

'I don't live on hope alone,' Tej Singh replied as Ketaki. 'I take my reward beforehand. If you offer me something right now, I could help you capture Tej Singh. If not, go ahead with your own plans.'

Both Nazim and Ahmed practically jumped with excitement. 'If you deliver Tej Singh into our hands today we'll pay whatever you ask!' Nazim said.

'I won't take a paisa less than a thousand rupees. If it suits you, bring the money right now.'

'From where will I get so much money in the middle of the night?' Nazim replied. 'I promise, I'll give it to you tomorrow.'

'Don't give me that talk. I've told you that I take my payment in advance. I'm off!' Tej made as if to leave.

Nazim quickly stopped him. 'Why are you getting annoyed? If you can't trust us, wait here. We'll get the money.'

'All right. One of you must wait with me while the other fetches the money.'

'Ahmed will stay with you,' Nazim said, and hurried to get the money from Krur Singh.

Tej, as Ketaki, began to chat with Ahmed to while away the time. He took out a few green cardamoms from his bag and offered him some. The prospect of capturing Tej Singh had turned Ahmed giddy with delight. He swallowed them without a second thought. When his head began to swim, he realized he had fallen into another aiyaar's trap. He pulled out his dagger and fell on Tej. But Tej was too quick. He grabbed Ahmed's wrist and disarmed him at once.

Ahmed fell down unconscious. Tej Singh tied him up tightly and wrapped him in a sheet. He loaded the bundle on his back and set off for Naugarh, walking as fast as he could, lest Nazim return and follow him.

In the meantime, Nazim hurried to Krur Singh's apartments and shook him awake.

'Nazim! What's so urgent?' Krur Singh grumbled, sitting up.

Nazim told him everything—how he had gone to Chandrakanta's garden and was captured by Chapla, how Ahmed rescued him and finally how the two came upon Ketaki.

'She's offered to capture Tej Singh for a thousand rupees,' he said. 'This opportunity should not be missed, sahib.'

'Well done!' Krur Singh's mouth curled in a smile.

He jumped out of bed and took out some money from a chest. 'Here,' he said. 'But I'm coming too, to meet this woman.'

They hurried to the spot where Nazim had left Ketaki and Ahmed, but found it deserted.

'Are you sure this is the place?' Krur asked.

Nazim nodded, his face wooden. 'I fear . . . we've been tricked,' he said.

'What do you mean?'

'It seems . . .' Nazim hung his head, 'it wasn't the real Ketaki. Probably an aiyaar who has taken Ahmed away.'

'Wonderful!' Krur exclaimed. 'You got a nice beating from Chapla. No doubt Ahmed is getting a dose too, right now.

Well, that's the end of your schemes.'

Nazim searched the neighbourhood for while, but there was no trace of them at all. The two men turned back, cursing.

The Secret Prison

Prince Virendra was in a pitiable state. His feelings for Chandrakanta overpowered him so much that nothing else seemed to exist. He spent his time sighing and bewailing his fate. Maharaja Surendra Singh well knew why his son was so dejected. But Chandrakanta's father was a much more powerful ruler than him, so he could only watch helplessly.

Virendra had given strict instructions to Tej to return the very same day. When midnight came and there was no sign of Tej, he was beside himself. He tried to sleep but could only toss and turn. Again and again, his eyes turned anxiously to the door.

Day was about to break when Tej appeared at last, carrying a bundle on his back. The palace guards were astonished at the sight but dared not utter a word, knowing how close he was to the prince.

Virendra sprang up from bed at once. 'What news?' he asked.

Tej Singh produced Chandrakanta's letter. Then he opened the bundle and said, 'There's your letter and here's a gift!' And he narrated the night's events.

Virendra's face lit up. He read and re-read the letter, touched it to his eyes, then said, 'You'd better confine Ahmed in a place so secret that no one gets the slightest hint. If Jai Singh finds out, the matter will become even more complicated.'

'I've already thought about it,' Tej replied. 'I'll take him to a cavern in the hills. No one knows of its existence, apart from me.'

He bundled Ahmed up again and asked a guard to fetch his friend Devi Singh. Devi was not only his friend and a distant relative, but Tej was training him to become an aiyaar.

'Let me carry the bundle, guruji,' Devi said, when he arrived.

He hoisted it on his shoulder and the two set off. Leaving the city behind them, they entered a dense forest. After walking almost four miles, they arrived at the opening of a dark narrow tunnel. When they had gone a short distance, they glimpsed light.

Tej halted. 'Put the bundle down,' he told Devi.

'This is a strange place, guruji,' Devi Singh frowned, removing his load. 'If anyone comes, it'll be impossible to escape.'

'Not a single soul knows about it,' Tej smiled. 'I brought you here only because I trust you. Also, I need your help—there are some difficult tasks ahead.'

'Well, you're my teacher,' Devi folded his hands. 'You've taught me all the tricks of our trade. I'll happily lay down my life for you.'

'Now listen carefully,' Tej said. 'See this stone door? I'm the only one who knows how to open it. There was someone else—my teacher, who trained me in the arts of the aiyaar. But he's no more. It's the right place to imprison people like Ahmed, and I plan to bring plenty more here. There's no need to tie them up, because it's not possible to get out. Inside, there is a stream that provides water to drink and lots of fruit trees, so our prisoners will not starve.'

Devi's eyes widened. 'What an extraordinary place!' he cried.

'It is,' Tej replied. 'Devi, I'm counting on you. There's much to do. You must ask his majesty for a month's leave, say you're ill. I'll put in a word on your behalf. You have to go to Vijaygarh and keep an eye on what's going on there—in disguise, of course. Keep me informed and whenever you get a chance to capture any of our enemies, deposit them here.'

'Just as you wish, guruji,' Devi said.

'Now follow my instructions and open the door,' Tej Singh said. A lion's head was carved on top of the door. Its mouth was wide open. 'Put your hand inside,' Tej instructed, 'and pull its tongue hard.'

Devi tugged at the lion's tongue till it hung out a whole

hand's length. They heard a loud, grinding noise and the door slid open. The aiyaars entered, carrying the bundled up Ahmed.

Inside was a meadow, almost two miles in length. Tall hills, that seemed too steep for anyone to climb, surrounded it. A small waterfall flowed in the middle and fruit-bearing trees clustered around, adding an idyllic charm to the place. Ber, gooseberries and chiraunji grew profusely, and huge rocks stood around like quiet elephants. The sound of the waterfall was soothing, as was the breeze rustling the trees, along with the cries of peacocks. A little stream curved from the west to the east, and jamun trees hung over it, dropping ripe purple fruit into the flowing water. The water was so clear that the bed of the stream was visible even though its depth reached the level of a man's waist in parts. The surrounding hills were full of little caves, as if nature had built small rooms for visitors to stay. With patches of clouds hanging over the hills like delicate white awnings, the place seemed so charming that one could spend years here, without feeling confined or unhappy.

The sun had come up now. Tej let Ahmed out of the bundle. He removed his dagger first, then the bag of tricks at his waist. Finally, he shackled one of his legs before bringing him back to consciousness.

Ahmed blinked and looked around him, 'Ah, am I dead? Have the angels brought me to paradise?' Immediately, he began to pray.

Tej couldn't help laughing. 'My dear fellow, you're not in heaven. You're our prisoner!'

Ahmed turned. His face shrivelled as he recognized Tej. Fear clutched his throat in such a tight grip that he couldn't utter a single word.

Tej smiled. 'Come,' he said to Devi. 'I think our prisoner will be fine in paradise.'

The aiyaars left Ahmed by the stream and went to the door. 'Push the lion's tongue back into its mouth,' Tej told Devi.

The moment he did so, the door slid shut. The two retraced their steps over the winding path and returned home.

The morning was well advanced by the time they reached the palace.

'What took you so long?' Virendra asked. 'Where have you imprisoned Ahmed?'

'In a grotto in the hills,' Tej replied. 'I'll take you there later. But I have a suggestion. Devi should be sent to Vijaygarh in disguise so he can keep watch and report to us. It will be very useful for us in our mission . . .'

Virendra nodded. 'My father's holding court,' he said. 'Let's go ask him.'

The three reached the court and at an appropriate moment, Devi made a request for one month's leave. At first the maharaja was unwilling, but when Virendra and Tej both pleaded his case, he agreed. After some preparation, Devi was sent to Vijaygarh.

The next day, Tej took Virendra to the valley where Ahmed was being kept captive and showed him how to open the door. The prince was enchanted with it.

'This grotto is surely a remarkable place!' he said.

'I was even more astounded than you when I first saw it,' Tej said. 'But my guruji told me that there was far more to it than met the eye. Some day we will explore it at greater length and discover those wonders.'

'Now that you've made such excellent arrangements, I'm tempted to attack Vijaygarh and carry Chandrakanta off,' Virendra confided, when they returned home.

'It's wonderful that you're feeling so confident,' Tej smiled. 'But you might put Chandrakanta at risk. Let me first go and see how they have reacted to Ahmed's disappearance.'

'I'm coming too,' Virendra frowned. 'I refuse to sit at home like a coward.'

'Well, then you should tell your father that you wish to go hunting for five or six days. We'll camp on the Vijaygarh border. The palace is barely five miles from there.'

'That's an excellent idea!' Virendra exclaimed.

The moment they got back, he went and asked his father for permission and got it. Accompanied by a retinue of his most loyal men, they left and set up camp on the border of Naugarh and Vijaygarh.

A Narrow Escape

When he discovered that Tej Singh had captured Ahmed, Nazim became very alarmed. Krur Singh too got concerned about his safety. He was constantly on the alert. Not that it deterred him from going to Jai Singh's court and reviling Virendra.

He was so obsessed with the thought of grabbing the throne of Vijaygarh that when Nazim suggested the only way to further his ambitions was by murdering his own father, he readily agreed. The king would surely make Krur Singh the prime minister in his father's place, Nazim argued, and once he had reached that position of power it would be easy to accomplish his aim of taking over the throne.

Consequently, one night when his father was about to

retire, Krur appeared with a glass of milk. 'I've noticed that you're neglecting your health, Pitaji,' he said. 'Please don't forget to have your glass of milk at night.' Kupath Singh was overjoyed to see his son's concern. He took the glass and drank up the milk. Within minutes he was writhing on the ground. Krur first disposed of the evidence, then began to wail and beat his breast. Soon there was pandemonium in the house.

Even though it was late, the news had to sent to Maharaja Jai Singh. The king was in his chambers, changing his clothes. 'Kupath Singh, dead?' he cried, sinking into a chair. 'Oh, how will I bear this loss!' It was such a great blow for the king that he did not attend court for several days. The whole city was plunged into mourning. Krur Singh pretended to be grief-stricken too. He stayed away from work for the twelve days of mourning. But all this time he was busy plotting with Nazim to get Tej and Virendra out of the way and marry Chandrakanta.

When he learned that Virendra had set up camp on the border of Vijaygarh, Nazim informed Krur immediately. 'He's definitely come to meet Chandrakanta,' he said. 'Oh . . . if only Ahmed were here. He would have found a way to foil his designs. Well . . . let's see what I can do.' He took leave of Krur and set out to scout the land.

However, Tej already knew their plans through the spies he had planted in the kingdom. He informed Virendra of the turn of events. 'It seems that in order to improve his chances of marrying Chandrakanta and grabbing the throne of

Vijaygarh, Krur has put his father out of the way. I have heard that when the period of mourning is over in another two days, Jai Singh intends to make him his prime minister.'

'What a monster!' Virendra shook his head. 'He can go to any extent to further his ambitions! I wouldn't be surprised if Jai Singh is his next victim.'

'The wretch will definitely turn on the king as soon as he finds an opportunity.' Tej pursed his mouth. 'Instead of checking out Chandrakanta's palace, I'm going to concentrate on getting information about the court. Of course, when I get a chance I'll look out for what's going on there, too.'

'I don't care about anything else,' Virendra said. 'Come what may, I'm going to try and meet Chandrakanta today.'

'Don't be so hasty. It might create problems.'

Tej tried his best to convince Virendra. But his words had no effect on the prince. 'I will go, come what may!' he said, squaring his shoulders and rising.

'All right,' Tej sighed. 'If that's what you want. We'll just have to face the consequences.'

That evening, the two set off for a stroll. They told their attendants not to worry if they got late returning. Walking in a leisurely manner, they made their way towards Vijaygarh.

It was already dark when they neared the garden where Chandrakanta often took the air in the evening. Since it was a moonless night, it was not very hard to enter. They managed to evade the guards easily. Tej flung a rope over the wall which both climbed up and quickly jumped into the garden.

They crept under a thickly foliaged tree and looked around.

Something caught their attention immediately. It was a lamp set on a marble platform, shedding a soft glow, right in the middle of the garden. Chandrakanta, Chapla and Champa were seated on that very platform, deep in conversation. Chapla's eyes darted around constantly, even as she talked.

When he set eyes on Chandrakanta, Virendra began to tremble. He was so overcome that he almost fainted away. Tej hurriedly produced a bottle of smelling salts from his bag of tricks and put it under his friend's nose.

'My dear prince,' he said, 'this is the worst place to lose control. Now take hold of yourself and wait here. I'll go and talk to them first, then escort you there.'

Tej left Virendra under the tree and headed towards the spot where the princess was sitting with the two girls.

'Well, sir, where have you been all these days?' Chandrakanta said. 'What kind of devotion is this? And again you've turned up alone. You might as well give up bragging about his bravery. If he is such a laggard in love, my life is of no use!'

Tears poured from her eyes and a storm of sobs convulsed her slender frame.

'This is what they call being childish,' Tej said, worried. 'You didn't even ask how he is—began crying instead. All right, if things are that bad, I'll fetch him right away.'

More tears flowed when Virendra and Chandrakanta came face to face.

'You've forgotten me!' she cried, jerking her head away.

'May I die, if I ever do so,' Virendra replied, going down on his knees. 'How I've longed for this moment!'

While the lovers were exchanging affectionate reproaches, Nazim happened to creep into the garden. His brow blackened with rage at the sight of this happy reunion. He turned and headed for Krur Singh's apartments at once.

'What's the matter?' Krur said, as he burst in. 'You look disturbed.'

'There's reason to be,' Nazim replied. 'It's turned out just as I thought. If we cannot make good use of this opportunity, you will lose everything.'

'What are you talking about?' Krur Singh asked.

'Prince Virendra is in the garden with Chandrakanta right now and the two are billing and cooing like a pair of lovesick doves.'

Krur turned white as a sheet. He sat there, looking like a frog, his head shaved, as he was pretending to mourn his father's death. He was not supposed to leave the house for thirteen days, but this news threw all such niceties out of his mind. He rushed to the king, his naked head shining like a water pot.

'What's this, Krur?' Jai Singh said, flabbergasted. 'Why have you hurried here, in this state? You're in mourning.'

'Maharaj, you are like a father to me,' Krur shed crocodile tears. 'Pitaji gave me birth but you brought me up. When I discovered that your honour was being compromised, I couldn't control myself. Of what use is my existence if I cannot serve you sincerely?'

'Who dares to do such a thing?' Jai Singh's face reddened with rage.

'There is one man,' Krur replied.

'Who is it? Tell me quickly.' Jai Singh ground his teeth. 'Who is this man who invites his death?'

'Virendra Singh.'

'He wouldn't dare to face me,' Jai Singh said, 'leave alone try to bring disrepute to my name. Quick, tell me clearly. Where is Virendra Singh?'

'In the garden of your Chormahal,' Krur said.

The moment he heard this, Jai Singh's body trembled with fury. 'Go and surround the garden immediately,' he ordered. 'I'll make my way through the fort.'

*

Virendra and Chandrakanta were still lost in each other. And Tej was exchanging pleasantries with Chapla. Poor Champa was gazing at the two pairs of lovers, feeling quite left out.

All of a sudden a man sprang on to the scene. He was dark as ebony, his eyes red as hot coals, with only a loincloth tied around his waist. He showed his teeth in a broad grin, then said to Tej, 'Listen master, the king knows all about you.' Then he leapt into the air and vanished. As he was leaving, he grabbed Champa's leg and dragged her for a short distance. Champa screamed, terrified. The others were startled out of their wits too!

But Tej rose and caught hold of the prince's hand. 'We must leave at once. You cannot stay here any longer!'

He turned to Chandrakanta and said, 'You mustn't weep over our sudden departure. All three of you, sit here calmly till the king comes.'

'But why are you leaving so soon?' Chandrakanta asked. 'Who was that fellow whose words make you flee?'

'There's no time for conversation,' Tej replied shortly.

He pulled Virendra away and, using the same rope, they vaulted over the garden walls without delay.

Chandrakanta turned to Chapla with tears in her eyes. 'What's all this?' she said. 'Why did they have to go? That demon was so terrifying—see, my heart is still pounding.'

'I really don't know what to say,' Chapla frowned. 'But I can guess this much—someone has informed his majesty that Virendra is here. He'll be arriving soon.'

'God knows what that wretch had against me,' Champa burst out suddenly.

Chapla couldn't help laughing. Totally confounded, the three tried to make sense of this strange turn of events. Then they heard loud voices all around them.

'This is a bad state of affairs,' Chapla looked around anxiously. 'Soldiers have surrounded the garden!' The words were barely out of her mouth when they saw the king coming towards them.

All three rose respectfully. Chandrakanta bowed to her

father. 'What brings you here in such haste?' she began, then stopped and fell silent.

'Nothing. Just wanted to see you. Come inside, child. Why are you sitting here at this late hour? There's dew falling. You'll get sick.'

He turned back towards the palace. The three girls followed him.

Once they were inside, Jai Singh left them and swept into his room, fuming. 'That scoundrel Krur! Maligning my innocent daughter without cause,' he said to himself. 'God knows what got into the fool's head! To be bold enough to blacken her name! What'll the girl say if she comes to know? He must be punished so severely that he never dares to do such a thing again.' Immediately, he sent for an officer named Hari Singh and told him to produce Krur at once.

Hari Singh went out to search for Krur and found him with the troops, happily laying siege to the garden.

'You must come right away!' Hari said. 'His majesty has sent for you.'

Krur panicked. Why was the king calling him? Hadn't they caught the culprit?

'What is his majesty doing?' he asked the officer.

'He's just come from the palace. He seems to be in quite a rage,' the man replied.

Krur felt the ground slip under his feet. Shivering with fear, he presented himself before Jai Singh.

'Well, Krur!' the king said, looking him up and down. 'Is this your favourite pastime—casting slurs on my blameless daughter? Shaming me? What must all those men who've been ordered to surround the garden be thinking? Idiot, donkey, rascal! What made you think that Virendra was there?'

The king's eyes burned red with anger, his lips quivered.

Krur was overcome with terror. 'Nazim gave me this information,' he said, panicking. 'He's one of the men who guard the palace.'

'Call this Nazim!' the king ordered.

By the time Nazim arrived Jai Singh was so enraged that he was spluttering. 'What's this, fellow? How dare you spread these lies?'

Nazim had given up all hope of escaping with his life. 'Y-your m-majesty,' he stammered. 'I saw him with my own two eyes. He must have run away.'

Jai Singh could not control himself any longer. 'Two hundred strokes of the whip for Nazim and fifty for Krur! The next time they presume to do such a thing, their heads will be lopped off. You are not fit to be my minister, Krur.'

The two men's screams rang through the palace; still the king's fury was not assuaged. They were turned out, yet Jai Singh could not be at peace.

The moment Krur and Nazim got back home Krur burst out, 'I'm in disgrace—and all because of you! My position's gone. I even had to suffer a whipping. Ouch, how my back hurts! All because of you, fool!'

'No, it's because of you that I was whipped; I didn't need to do all this for myself,' Nazim replied. 'To hell with Chandrakanta and Virendra! I didn't deserve this beating.'

'Well, we're both fools,' Krur said finally, 'if after all this punishment, we can't get even with Virendra.'

'There's no doubt that he'll be visiting the palace every day now. Why else do you think he set up camp close by?' Nazim fumed. He shook his head hopelessly. 'But I don't feel like doing anything now. What if I report him and he slips off again? I'll surely pay with my life this time.'

'We have to think of a foolproof plan,' Krur chewed his moustache, then clicked his tongue irritably. 'Maharaja Jai Singh must discover Virendra himself.'

Nazim stroked his beard and narrowed his eyes. Several minutes ticked by before he spoke. 'There is a famous astrologer in Maharaja Shivdutt's court, the ruler of Chunar.'

'I know who he is,' Krur snapped. 'Get on with it!'

'Well, this Pandit Jagannath, he's so well versed in the art of divination that he can tell you everything—where a particular person is at a particular time, what he's doing, how he can be caught, anything. If we can persuade him to come here for a few days and help us, everything will work out. Chunar isn't too far from here, just about forty-six miles. Let's go and try to persuade him.'

'Now you're talking sense.' Krur's eyes gleamed. He opened a box, took out some jewels, tied them up in a silk handkerchief and tucked the bundle into his waist. Then he sent for two swift steeds and they left for Chunar.

'If Maharaj sends for me, say I'm too ill to get up,' he told the servant, who came to see him off. 'And tell everyone to stick to this story, all right?'

The servant nodded, too afraid to question him.

*

After leaving the garden, Virendra and Tej hurried back to their camp. It was past midnight when they reached. But how could Tej rest? He quickly made himself up to look like Ahmed and set off for Krur Singh's house. Krur had already left for Chunar by then.

The servants left behind to guard the house asked, astonished, 'Where have you been, Ahmed?'

'To hell and back!' said the sham Ahmed. 'Now tell me where they are.'

'They've gone to Chunar,' said one. 'Don't you know what happened?' The story was repeated. 'Better you go there too,' the man ended.

'You're right. I'll leave right away. I won't even go home.'

Tej returned to the camp and told Virendra what had happened. The next morning after a quick breakfast, he set off for Vijaygarh again.

Bareheaded, his face and body smeared with dust, he arrived at the court, wailing loudly. Everyone stared at him in surprise. The maharaja's clerk asked, 'Who are you and what do you want?'

'Your honour, I'm Krur Singh's servant, Ram Lakhan,' Tej said. 'He has turned against the king and gone off to Chunar. When I told him not to betray his majesty, he beat me up and grabbed whatever I had. What am I to do now? What'll I eat? How will I go home? My sons will ask, what did you earn at the court? What happened to your three years' savings? What will I give them? I want justice, your majesty, justice!'

With great difficulty, he was silenced. Furious, Jai Singh sent for Krur and was told that he was very sick.

'It's a lie, Maharaj!' Tej burst out again. 'I want justice, my lord. You must investigate.'

The maharaja told his clerk to go and find out. Krur Singh was discovered to be missing. His servants refused to disclose where he had gone. But after being beaten the poor fellows came out with it—Krur had left for Chunar.

Jai Singh flew into an uncontrollable rage. He ordered that everyone be turned out of Krur's house and his possessions looted. Then he proclaimed that Ram Lakhan could help himself to as much of Krur's wealth as he could carry. The rest would be deposited in the royal treasury. If Ram Lakhan wished he would be given a job at the court.

Tej dressed as Ram Lakhan hurried to Krur's house and clamoured for his share. The clerk tried to fob him off with just two thousand rupees, but he shouted and wailed so much that he let him take what he wanted. Tej stuffed money into his pockets, his moneybag, his turban and even into his mouth! In this way he made off with about ten thousand rupees.

The house was ransacked, and all its inhabitants set off for Chunar, lamenting and cursing their fate.

Tej Singh hurried to the camp and told Virendra, 'It's been a profitable day! But my friend, this is dirty money. If you add something to it, it'll get purified.'

'From where did you get it?'

Tej informed him. Virendra laughingly turned out his

moneybag and said, 'This is all I have here.'

'But I have a condition. You can't give less—your status is so much higher than Krur's.'

'I told you I'm cleaned out.'

'Then write a promissory note!'

The prince laughed even harder and removed the diamond ring from his finger.

Tej touched it to his eyes, saying, 'May God almighty grant all your wishes! But now we must go home because I must set off for Chunar and find out what that spawn of a devil is up to.'

*

The news of Krur's disgrace spread like wildfire through the city. Chandrakanta heard of it too, as did her mother Maharani Ratnagarbha.

When the king came to the palace, the queen jokingly inquired about Krur. 'He was a villain, a liar,' replied the king. 'He was maligning our daughter for no rhyme or reason.'

'But why did you stop Virendra from coming here?' The queen grabbed the opportunity. 'He's the very same boy who used to visit us even before Chandrakanta was born. He'd stay with us for several days and play with her when she was a baby. That's why the two love each other so much.' The queen paused and sighed deeply. 'At that time it felt as if you and Maharaja Surendra Singh were one, and Naugarh and Vijaygarh the same kingdom. Surendra Singh always followed your advice and you always said that Chandrakanta should marry Virendra. That despicable Krur destroyed your friendship and created distrust between you.'

'I'm flabbergasted myself.' The king looked away shamefaced. 'How did I lose all reason? What caused me to turn against Virendra? That Krur achieved the impossible. Now that he's gone, I realize how evil he was.'

'Well, let's see what he gets up to in Chunar,' replied the queen. 'He'll definitely instigate Maharaja Shivdutt against us and create fresh problems.'

'We'll have to deal with that,' the king's mouth drooped. 'May God be witness, the rogue did not leave anything undone in his villainy.'

Jai Singh left the palace lost in thought. He was concerned about finding a new prime minister now. After several days of deliberation, he appointed a junior officer named Hardayal Singh. He was an honest, upright and good-hearted person, who had never harmed anyone.

Krur's Revenge

One thought obsessed Krur Singh now—how to get rid of Virendra and Tej Singh and destroy the kingdom of Naugarh. He arrived in Chunar with Nazim and presented himself at the court of Maharaja Shivdutt, armed with a suitable gift.

The king knew him well. He accepted the offering and said, 'And how are things with you?'

'Whatever they be,' Krur replied, 'I will inform you in private, Maharaj.'

Shivdutt sent for Krur in the evening, when the court had been dismissed. 'So, what is it you wish to tell me?' he asked.

'I have been treated atrociously by Jai Singh,' Krur said. 'Humiliated, even whipped for no fault. This is a golden opportunity for you, your majesty. I have plenty of supporters in Vijaygarh. The king's army is in disarray. If you were inclined, we could easily defeat him and occupy his kingdom. Better still, you could claim his daughter Chandrakanta, an incomparable beauty, as the spoils of war.'

Shivdutt smiled and nodded. Krur continued to persuade him that Vijaygarh was ripe for plucking.

Finally, the ruler said, 'I don't perceive any need to go into battle right now. I'll send four of my six excellent aiyaars with you to do the spadework first, along with Pandit Jagannath, the astrologer. At a suitable time, I'll follow with my forces.'

He sent for his aiyaars—Pandit Badrinath, Pannalal, Chunnilal, Ram Narayan, Bhagwandutt and Ghasita Singh—and instructed four of them to accompany Krur.

They were still discussing their strategy, when a guard arrived. 'Your majesty,' he said, ' a group of supplicants is at your door. They claim to be relatives of Krur Singh and are saying that when Jai Singh heard Krur Singh had come here, he turned them all out and ransacked his house. What shall I tell them?'

Krur Singh froze immediately. His face turned ashen.

'Send them in,' said the king.

After the whole story had been told, one of the servants said, looking at Krur and Nazim, 'But sahib, hasn't Ahmed reached here?'

'Ahmed? Where is he?' Nazim exclaimed. 'He certainly didn't come here!'

'But he arrived at the house and said that he would join you at Chunar!'

Nazim's face darkened. 'I know who it was. That scoundrel, Tej Singh! He must have gone and informed Jai Singh. He's responsible for all this.'

Hearing this, Krur broke down and wept bitterly.

'There's no point bewailing what has happened,' Shivdutt said. 'Wait and see how I get even with Jai Singh. You can stay here for the time being, along with your dependents. There's a vacant house in front of the public baths. I'll provide money for your needs.'

Krur Singh took up residence in that house. After a few days, he presented himself in court again and asked for leave to go to Vijaygarh. All the preparations had been made and the four aiyaars were fully equipped. They took a variety of clothing for their disguises, hung bags of tricks on their shoulders and tucked daggers into their waists. Pandit Jagannath took his books and other tools of divination, apart from the aiyaar's kit, since he was somewhat familiar with that art too. The group had plans to visit Naugarh as well.

Masters of Disguise

Virendra and Tej Singh were sitting outside the fort of Naugarh, on the banks of the Chandraprabha River, enjoying the view, along with a large retinue. The river was very wide at that spot. A dense forest of sakhu faced them on the opposite bank and the cries of thousands of peacocks and black-faced monkeys clamoured in their ears.

But the separation from Chandrakanta filled Prince Virendra with gloom. The peacocks' cries felt like arrows piercing his heart, the monkeys' calls like rocks flung at him. Even the pleasant evening breeze seared him like the scorching summer loo. He sat there watching the river silently, attempting to relieve his agony with deep sighs.

Suddenly a sadhu came into view. Dressed in saffron with a tilak on his forehead, he was carrying a khanjari—a pair of musical tongs—in his hands. He sat down on the bank at a distance and began to sing:

'Chameleon Krur to Chunar went and fetched four aiyaars
With them a saintly pandit, who can foretell omens far
Caution's the word—there's much he can divine
Don't sit here careless, up, up—arise and shine!'

Tej sat up and stared at the man. The sadhu nodded and grinned, showing all his teeth. Then he rose and went on his way.

Lost in thoughts of Chandrakanta, Virendra failed to notice anything. He did not even look up to see who was singing or where the sound came from. Transfixed, he sat there, gazing at the river. When Tej shook his arm, he came to with a start.

'Did you hear anything?' Tej asked in an undertone.

'What? No, tell me,' replied the prince.

'Get up, let's go to your room. This has to be discussed in private,' Tej said.

The two made their way to the fort. When they were safe in Virendra's private chamber, he asked, 'What is it?'

'Well, you know that Krur Singh went to Chunar,' Tej said. 'It seems Shivdutt has provided him with four aiyaars and a pandit skilled at divination. Along with Nazim, he has a strong group of supporters. Now, I have to leave for work.

I'm sure one of them will come here and try to dupe you. Please be on your guard. If anyone offers you any flowers or perfume to smell, keep away! And don't go anywhere with anyone. Someone might turn up impersonating me. There's a way to check—I have a black spot inside my lower eyelid. Even if I come here in disguise, I'll show it to you quietly. So please, don't trust anyone.'

'But how did you find out?' asked the prince.

'I have ways,' Tej smiled. 'And if the king or my father asks for me, kindly think of an excuse.'

Tej then whipped out the tools of his trade, double-checked to see if everything was there, and took to the road.

*

At the very same time, Chapla decided to go scouting, dressed as a man. It was past midnight when she left, and the clear, bright moonlight stirred a thought in her head: to head towards Naugarh and seek Tej.

As chance would have it, the two ran into each other en route. Chapla had no problem identifying him. Tej had not bothered to change his appearance. She simply approached him and asked in her natural voice, 'Where are you off to?'

Tej recognized her at once. 'Wah, what luck!' he said. 'I had many important things to discuss with you. It would have been hard to locate you otherwise.'

He beckoned her to take a seat on a flat rock nearby.

'What do you wish to talk about?' Chapla asked.

'You know that Krur's at Chunar,' Tej began. 'He's coming back with a band of four aiyaars and an accomplished astrologer. They have already reached, in fact. We are severely outnumbered—just the two of us against that large group. I wouldn't be surprised if they try to carry Maharaja Jai Singh himself off. And they've definitely got plans for Chandrakanta. I was coming to warn you.'

'So, how can we foil them?'

'I'm thinking of adopting your prime minister's persona. That way I'll be able to achieve much. I want you to be on the lookout too, and meet me at least once every day.'

After some further talk, Chapla turned back to the palace. Tej Singh spent the rest of the night in the forest. Next morning he disguised himself as a perfume seller. With a bag of scent bottles at his waist and a couple in his hand, he set off for Vijaygarh and began to roam the streets.

In the evening, when he felt the time was right, he arrived at Hardayal's house. The minister was sprawled on his dewan and a couple of friends sat there, gossiping. The house was deserted otherwise.

Tej Singh salaamed him respectfully. 'I come from Lucknow, your honour,' he said. 'I heard that you are a connoisseur of fine goods, so I brought my choicest attars for you.' He opened a bottle and dabbed a little scent on a wad of cotton wool.

Hardayal accepted it graciously, sniffed at the perfume and passed it around his friends. Within moments, they were all unconscious. Tej quickly bundled the minister in a sheet and sped to Naugarh, his face hidden under a cloth. Thinking he was a washerman, no one challenged him.

He carried the minister to the cave where he had imprisoned Ahmed. He removed Hardayal's signet ring and his clothes. Then he made himself up as Hardayal and hurried back to Vijaygarh.

He found the minister's house in a state of turmoil. When his maid came to serve dinner, she found all the friends knocked out flat and no sign of her master. She set up a hue and cry. The other servants searched for him, panic-stricken, but without success. Finally his companions came to and told them about the perfume seller. The night passed in speculation and they were still wondering where to look for the minister, when he was glimpsed heading towards the house.

Immediately he was bombarded with questions: 'Where were you?' 'What happened?'

'That man was a proper crook.' Hardayal shook his head. 'I sensed something fishy, so I didn't inhale the scent. When you people began to pass out, I ran after him. I followed him for a long distance, but the rascal got away.'

'Oh, sahib, won't you eat something?' asked the maid.

'No, I'm very tired. I'll lie down for a while.'

The friends left exclaiming at the strange occurrence.

Tej had studied Hardayal's habits. At the usual time, he set off for court, returning the greetings of passers-by with a slight nod. The king had not arrived, so he sat down and began to study the papers placed there for the minister.

After a while, Jai Singh appeared and the day's work began. Tej waited for a quiet moment, then said softly, 'Your majesty, I have heard from reliable sources that Maharaja Shivdutt has provided Krur with four aiyaars and they are headed this way to create trouble for you. It seems he has even said that he will follow with an army.' He paused, then continued, 'Now the biggest problem is that our two aiyaars Nazim and Ahmed went with Krur and there's no one else left. Those men might already be here, roaming around in disguise. It appears too, that Krur has supporters here.'

'I'm well aware that Krur has supporters here,' replied the king. 'But what are we doing to counter them?'

Tej's eye suddenly fell on a guard who stood there watching them slyly. He stared back and the guard seemed to collect himself.

'Bring that fellow here,' Tej rapped out, pointing to the man. The moment the other guards turned towards him, the fellow took to his heels. Tej could have caught him easily. But as Hardayal, he had to act like a minister.

So he simply turned to the king and said, 'Did you see that, Maharaj? What I feared has come true!'

Jai Singh rose, perturbed. He dismissed the court and went into his private chamber, beckoning to Tej to come with him.

'What should we do now? That scoundrel Krur has created a powerful enemy for us. We cannot match Shivdutt in any way.' The king paced up and down agitatedly.

'Your majesty, I'll repeat what I had said earlier. We do

not possess a good aiyaar to counter theirs. Only someone skilled in this art can foil them. An aiyaar works silently and can even put a thousand men out of commission,' Tej said. 'I hear that Tej Singh, the son of Maharaja Surendra Singh's prime minister, has turned out to be a master of this art. I'm also hopeful that the king of Naugarh will come to your aid if you ask him. You may have stopped Virendra from coming here, but his father still holds you in high esteem.'

Jai Singh remained silent for a while, lost in deep thought. 'You are right,' he said finally. 'Maharaja Surendra Singh and Virendra are both good people. Virendra is brave enough to fight ten thousand with an army of a thousand men. And Tej Singh is as wily as you say. But I have wronged them so grievously that I don't have the face to ask them for any favours. How can they consider me a friend now? If you could go and smooth things over, I'd be grateful.'

'There can't be a better suggestion, Maharaj,' Tej Singh said. 'If you would write a letter and stamp it with your seal, I'll leave right away. And it'll be best if I go alone.'

The plan appealed to the king. Immediately he dashed off a letter, stamped it with his signet ring and handed it to the minister.

The false Hardayal went home. He did not enter the women's quarters though, and had his meal in an outer room. Then he thought it was time to confer with Chapla. By chance, she arrived, just as dusk was falling. She was pleased to hear what had transpired and said, 'Hardayal would definitely support your plan. Hurry now, and accomplish this quickly.'

Tej started off for Naugarh, adopting his real form on the way.

*

Naugarh and Vijaygarh both lay amidst lush green hills. The rivers Chandraprabha and Karamnasa wound through the kingdoms. The hills were dotted with caves and tunnels and covered with forests so dense that a traveller could easily lose his way. Villages lay in between these forests. In the rainy season scores of little brooks gurgled through the pathways. Many wild animals and birds inhabited these forests too. Tigers and leopards, bears and several kinds of deer and monkeys could be found, along with peacocks and partridge and quail.

The Chunar aiyaars decided to camp here with Krur, and set out separately for work. When they needed each other, they would return and as a signal, whistle in a special way. The most cunning, Badrinath, proposed that they enter the city and the court in disguise and study the speech and gait of all the important people, among them the queen, princess and her attendants, so that they could easily pass off as these people when they impersonated them. Disguised as Chapla and Champa, once even as the princess, they managed to enter the palace a few times. But Chapla almost caught Nazim when he was trying to pass off as Chandrakanta, and he was compelled to flee. Alarmed, they decided to concentrate on spying out the land, and not take unnecessary risks.

Finally, Bhagwandutt felt confident enough to disguise

himself as Chapla and arrived in Naugarh to gull Prince Virendra. It was already quite dark and the prince was seated in his chambers, dreaming of Chandrakanta as usual, when the guard came and told him that Chapla was at the door, asking to meet him.

The prince started up joyfully. 'Send her in at once!' he said.

As soon as she entered, he rose, took her hand and made her sit down. 'And how's my beloved?' he asked eagerly.

'She's all right. But she misses you each and every moment of the day. "How uncaring he is!" she keeps saying. "He doesn't even send to ask if I'm alive or dead." Today she was so agitated that she asked me to bring these pears for you, which she peeled and cut up herself. She asked that you eat them for her sake.'

Virendra was overcome with happiness. Forgetting Tej's warnings, he reached out and was about to put a piece into his mouth, when his friend entered. He took in the whole scene and burst out angrily, 'Stop! Don't put that into your mouth!'

The prince halted, confused. 'Why, what's wrong?'

'I broke my head, cautioning you a hundred times over. Still it didn't sink into your brain. Has Chapla ever come here earlier? Couldn't you make sure if it actually *was* her? This female wormed her way in with her sweet talk and you fell for it!'

Virendra flushed. He examined the impostor with narrowed eyes. Exposed, the aiyaar pulled out his dagger and leapt on Tej. But Virendra was quicker. He grabbed his wrist and putting his other arm around the man's waist, lifted him above his head and was about to hurl him to the ground.

'Stop! Don't kill him, hand him over to me.' Tej cried. 'He was just doing his job.' The prince let the man down lightly, then tied up his wrists. Tej stuffed some knock-out medicine into his nostrils, bundled him up and set him aside.

'Well, that's done!' Tej wiped his brow, then let out a long exasperated breath. 'Please, for heaven's sake, be careful now.'

Virendra went red. Instead of replying, he asked, 'And how're things in Vijaygarh?'

Tej reported all that had happened. Then he took out the letter Maharaja Jai Singh had sent.

Virendra jumped up and embraced him in a bear hug. 'Hurry!' he said. 'Do what you need to quickly!'

Tej smiled. 'Don't get so worked up,' he said, stretching leisurely. 'Everything will fall into place.'

They spent the night making plans. Before the first pale light of day appeared, Tej hoisted the bundle on his back and stepped on to the path that led to his cave prison.

Ahmed was sound asleep near the spring. But Hardayal Singh sat on a rock under a tree, his head bent low with gloom. He rose at once when he saw Tej. 'What crime have I committed Tej,' he said reproachfully, 'that you have confined me here?'

Tej bowed low. 'Your honour, if you had been guilty of a crime, wouldn't I have shackled you like Ahmed?' he smiled. 'Please forgive me for being so discourteous. I needed to keep you out of the way for just one day. You are free to go where you wish. There is no one as honest and just-minded as you in Vijaygarh and I dearly need your help.'

Hardayal's face brightened. 'I have always held you and the prince in high esteem. That's why I was shocked to find you had imprisoned me. In fact, I wouldn't have known how I got here if I hadn't seen Ahmed. Now tell me why this was necessary and how I can help you.'

Tej gazed at the ground. 'I want to assure you that I didn't enter your ladies' apartments.'

Hardayal laughed. 'You are more than a son to me. What difference would it make if you had? Tell me, anyway.'

Tej first returned his clothes, then gave him the king's letter. 'Now please get ready and come to Naugarh with me. You must ask the king to let me accompany you. Else those aiyaars will destroy Vijaygarh. And please keep reminding Maharaja Jai Singh that Virendra wishes him well, so he's encouraged to ask him for help.'

'I promise I'll do much more than you ask,' Hardayal swore fervently.

But first Tej had to unwrap his prize. He shackled the impostor, then removed his bag and dagger. Then he washed his face and discovered it was Bhagwandutt, whom he had known of earlier. Leaving him by the stream, he exited the cave with the minister.

'I'm afraid I'll have to put you out again,' he said.

'Do what you wish. I have no desire to learn the way to this place.'

Once they had left the grotto, Tej restored Hardayal to

consciousness. The prime minister dressed in his own clothes and on reaching the city, they parted ways. Hardayal set off for Surendra Singh's court. He was received with great respect and Jeet Singh read out the letter.

'My kingdom belongs to Jai Singhji,' said the monarch. 'He can invite whom he wants. Take Tej with you.'

But before they left, Jeet Singh insisted on entertaining Hardayal lavishly for three days while the king loaded him with gifts of cash and jewels. Then he started out for Vijaygarh along with Tej.

Jai Singh was overjoyed when Tej was presented at the evening durbar. He commanded that the aiyaar receive proper accommodation and all the amenities possible.

A Game of Wits

Now Tej Singh was eager to find out which of Shivdutt's aiyaars was roving the city. He made himself up as Bhagwandutt, and set out for the forest, convinced that the party would be camping there. However, after scouring the place for a long time, he did not find anyone. It was a typical monsoon night, dark and cloudy. In the end he climbed to the top of a hillock and whistled, hoping to get some response.

As he expected, three aiyaars appeared, along with Pandit Jagannath. 'You'd gone to Naugarh,' they said. 'Why have you come back empty handed?'

'Tej Singh scuttled all my plans,' Tej shrugged, examining them slyly. 'If one of you had accompanied me, things would have been different.'

'I will tomorrow,' Pannalal said. 'But right now let's go to the palace and try our luck.'

'All right. But I'm ravenous,' Tej replied.

'Well, all the food we have is doctored,' Jagannath said. 'Why don't you go to the market and get something for everyone.'

'As you say. But one of you must come along.'

Pannalal agreed. When they were close to the city he said, 'We need to disguise ourselves. I've heard that Tej Singh is here. He recognizes all of us.'

'Oh, who'll be able to make out in the dark,' Tej said quickly, apprehensive that he might be exposed while they made themselves up.

Pannalal threw him a suspicious look. It was too dark to make out anything, still he whistled for his companions. But they were too far away to hear. Tej guessed that his disguise had been penetrated and grabbed him from behind. Pannalal drew his dagger immediately. The two scuffled for a while but finally Tej overpowered him. He made Pannalal unconscious, bundled him up and set off for the city. There he restored his own appearance and went to his quarters.

Confining the aiyaar in another room, he went to bed. The next day he presented him in court.

*

Pannalal's companions waited for a long time. Suspecting that the two might have got caught, they headed for the city

59

in the morning, well disguised. There they caught sight of Tej, with Pannalal trailing behind him, surrounded by guards. They decided to follow them.

The court was packed and Jai Singh already seated on his throne. Tej salaamed the king and pushed Pannalal before him.

'Who have you brought, Tej?' asked the king.

'Maharaj, this is one of the four aiyaars from Chunar. I've captured him for you. Please tell me what should be done with him.'

'Well done!' Jai Singh said, elated. He studied the aiyaar. 'What's your name, fellow?' he asked.

'Makkar Khan, alias Aiyaar Khan!' Pannalal replied.

Jai Singh couldn't help laughing at his impertinence and quick wittedness. 'There's no need to question this fellow too much,' he said. 'Take him to the dungeons and lock him up. And see that he's guarded well.'

The guards shackled Pannalal and took him away. Then the king rewarded Tej with a hundred asharfis. Tej salaamed him deeply and promptly stowed the coins in his moneybag.

The other aiyaars witnessed all this. When Pannalal received his sentence, they hurriedly left to deliberate. Then Badrinath swiftly made himself up to look like Tej, while the others affected the soldiers' appearance.

They caught up with the guards and Badrinath said, 'Wait a minute. His majesty has sent other orders for this wicked fellow. He's asked me to keep him in my own custody, lest his comrades try to free him.'

The guards knew that Tej had captured him, so they willingly surrendered the prisoner. For a while they followed the group as they headed towards the forest. Then they returned to court to inform the king that they had followed his orders.

When they saw Tej Singh seated there, they were dumbstruck.

'Did you lock that man up properly?' Tej asked.

'B-but, sahib,' the guards replied, shivering, 'you just took him away!'

Tej started up. 'What do you mean? I've been sitting here all the while!'

Flabbergasted, terrified, the guards did not know what to say; they just stood there, rooted.

'What's wrong?' asked the king.

Tej Singh had guessed what had happened. 'Your majesty, the other aiyaars managed to trick them. One of them disguised himself as me and took the prisoner away.'

'What are you saying?' the king replied, horrified. 'Why were you people so careless?'

'Don't scold them, your majesty. Aiyaars can fool the best of us,' Tej said.

Jai Singh was mollified, but the thought of this escape filled him with gloom.

*

Once the aiyaars were safe in the forest, they sat down under a tree to talk. It struck them now that Bhagwandutt might have fallen victim to Tej Singh.

'Why don't you find out where he has been confined?' Badrinath asked Pandit Jagannath.

The astrologer took out his tools, made some calculations, then said, 'Yes, Tej Singh has definitely caught him. He is imprisoned in a cave about four miles from here.'

The aiyaars immediately set off in that direction. With the help of his divining tools, Jagannath guided them to the correct place. But when they were confronted with the huge door, he said, 'There is a special method to open this door, which I cannot determine. We will have to find out somehow.'

Disappointed, the aiyaars left, vowing to discover the secret.

*

The next afternoon, Tej set off to scout the areas near Vijaygarh. He had gone a long distance, when he saw Virendra seated under a tree. His horse was tied to another tree and a freshly slaughtered deer lay nearby. A fire smouldered close to it and some pieces of flesh were placed on large flat leaves.

'Tej! Come here,' the prince called out. 'You've completely forgotten us, ever since you left for Vijaygarh.'

'And why did I go to Vijaygarh?' Tej laughed. 'On your business or my father's?'

'Your father's!' replied the prince, laughing. 'Now tell me,' he said as Tej sat down near him, 'Did you meet Chandrakanta?'

'I haven't had the time,' Tej replied. 'I captured an aiyaar but his companions impersonated me and set him free. No luck after that.'

'Those fellows are real devils,' said the prince.

'That they are. But the only one I fear is Badrinath. He's extremely wily. Well, we'll see about that. But what are you doing here all alone?'

'I had gone hunting with some of my men in the morning,' said the prince. 'But couldn't find any prey till the afternoon. Then I saw this stag. It led me such a merry chase that everyone was left behind. Finally, I brought it down with a well-placed arrow. I was so hungry that I couldn't wait to roast it. Now that you're here, why don't you start it off? I've added some masala to the meat. But be quick. I haven't eaten all day.'

Tej roasted the meat and the two sat down by a stream to eat. Virendra began to wipe the masala off before eating.

'Why are you doing that?' Tej asked.

'It's a bit too spicy for me,' he replied.

After eating two or three pieces, the prince drank deeply from the stream. 'I just can't eat any more,' he said. 'When you stay hungry the whole day, you feel full the moment you take a bite.'

'Well, whether you eat or not I'm going to finish it off. It's turned out really good.'

When he had finished, Tej washed his face and hands and said, 'I'll accompany you to Naugarh.'

But after walking a short distance, he put a hand to his head. 'Don't know why I'm feeling so dizzy.'

'Maybe you ate too much,' Virendra replied.

Suddenly Tej slumped to the ground, unconscious. Virendra quickly jumped off his horse, tied him up in a bundle and hoisted him over his back. He took the road that led to Vijaygarh. When he got to the forest, he whistled. In a short while Krur, Pannalal, Ramnarayan and the astrologer appeared.

'Badrinath, you've won a real prize for us,' Pannalal thumped him on the back.

Krur was so overjoyed that he danced around clapping his hands. The bogus Virendra—Badrinath—placed the bundle on the ground and directed Ramnarayan to return the horse to the Naugarh stables from where he had stolen it. He conferred with the others for a while, then picked Tej up again and set off for Chunar.

When Jai Singh found Tej missing from his usual seat at court for two consecutive days, he asked Hardayal where he was. The minister made enquiries at Tej's home but was told that he had not been seen for a few days. Worried, Hardayal sent men to search in the city, but they could not trace Tej Singh. Finally, he wrote a letter to Tej's father and despatched a trustworthy man to Naugarh, urging him to bring back a reply before the court gathered the next morning.

When Jeet Singh read the letter, he was convinced that his son had been captured by the Chunar aiyaars. He simply wrote, 'Tej Singh is not here,' on a piece of paper and gave it to the messenger.

The following day he approached Surendra Singh in

court. 'Maharaj, I received a letter from the prime minister of Vijaygarh asking if Tej was here. I replied, saying he was not.'

The king stared at him, perturbed. 'He's surely fallen into the hands of those Chunar aiyaars. He had gone to face them all alone.'

'I suppose we'll find out in a few days,' Jeet Singh said.

But Virendra was already on his feet. 'Please,' he asked his father, 'may I go and look for Tej?'

'We know how brave you are, your highness,' Jeet Singh said with a smile. 'But he has been captured by aiyaars, which means his life is not in danger. They must have imprisoned him somewhere. Clever as he is, he will surely manage to escape. The fact is, even the most cunning aiyaar can slip up sometime. If he doesn't return within the next ten days, please go ahead and do what you wish.'

'True, he is very sharp, but we must search all the same.' Anxiety creased Virendra's face.

'Your love for your friend is filling you with concern,' said the minister.

'Why don't you send someone to make enquires?' Surendra Singh suggested.

'Your majesty, I have already despatched some spies,' Jeet Singh replied.

The king and his son both fell silent, but remained preoccupied.

*

Matters were no different at the Vijaygarh court. As soon as he entered court, Jai Singh asked Hardayal if he had any information about Tej. Just then the messenger arrived with the news that he was not in Naugarh.

The king's face grew taut. 'Have you made any attempt to find out where he could be?' he asked.

'Yes, your majesty. Spies have been put on the job.'

But this answer did not satisfy Jai Singh. His face was overcast when he returned to his chambers in the palace that evening. 'This is what they describe as the vagaries of fortune,' he said to the queen. 'Krur Singh has created serious problems for us. And Tej, who came to our help, has vanished mysteriously. How will I face Surendra Singh?' He sighed deeply. 'What a charming boy he was, witty, quick and so adept at his craft. I've never seen him without a smile.'

'It is a great misfortune, indeed,' the queen shook her head. 'Pray to god, he is found soon.'

Chapla happened to be standing there. When she heard this, her heart plummeted. She hurried to Chandrakanta.

'What's the matter?' Chandrakanta cried. 'Why are you so upset? Tell me at once!'

Chapla's face was ashen, her lips quivered. She tried to speak but her throat choked up and tears began to stream from her eyes.

'Why are you crying? Why don't you tell me?'

Chapla pulled herself together somehow. 'I just heard Maharaj tell your mother that Tej has been captured by

Shivdutt's aiyaars. Now how will Virendra get here? Tej was helping him.' She burst out crying loudly.

At once Chandrakanta guessed that Chapla had fallen in love with Tej. She thought it was a good thing. But their sad situation aroused her sympathy. 'Have you no other plans to set him free? Will weeping get him out of their clutches? If you can't do anything, let me try.'

Champa sprang up, agitated. 'If you permit,' she said, 'I'll go and search for Tej!'

'You're not that proficient,' Chapla immediately wiped her tears. 'This is a job for an aiyaar.'

'So don't I know the art?' Champa cried.

'You do, but you are no match for the Chunar aiyaars. How cunningly they've captured an expert like Tej! If your highness agrees, I'll go and find him.'

'Why are you waiting for my permission? Go at once. If you set him free, he'll remember it all his life.'

Chapla turned to Champa. 'Take good care of the princess,' she said. 'Keep her safe from those wily aiyaars.'

She armed herself with her tools, along with clothes and jewellery in the style women from the Deccan wore. Then she set off.

Chapla the Aiyaara

Chapla was no ordinary woman. Her fragile beauty was deceptive. She was actually extremely strong. In fact, she was capable of grappling with two or three men at a time and getting the better of them. Besides being adept at the aiyaar's tricks, she was an accomplished singer and dancer and well versed in the art of making fireworks too. When she set off on work, she would deliberately cloak her looks or change her appearance.

Today, however, Chapla went out into the moonlit night undisguised, though she carried her bag and her dagger. Her anxiety had overcome her so that she was completely oblivious of the world around. Sobbing, almost blinded by her tears, she stumbled on, blundering into bushes, stubbing her feet on stones. It was only when she tumbled into a stream and split her head open that she came to her senses. Then she realized that she had lost her way and wandered into a particularly dark and fearsome part of the forest. With an effort, she mastered her panic and reminded herself that she had set out for a specific purpose. It struck her that the aiyaars might have taken Tej to Chunar. So she began to hunt for the road that led there. It was past midnight when she located it. When dawn broke, she dressed up as a soldier and continued her journey over the hills.

The next evening she arrived at Chunar. After wandering in the city for a while she realized that it would be hard to discover anything this way. So she made herself up to resemble Pannalal and asked for the way to Ghasita Singh's house. Ghasita was one of the aiyaars who had been kept back in Chunar.

He greeted her warmly. 'Well, Pannalal, who have you brought this time?' he asked.

'No one. I just came to ask if Nazim's here. We haven't seen him for two days.'

'He hasn't come here.'

'But who could have captured him? There are no aiyaars left there.'

'I'm not sure about that.' Ghasita scratched his head. 'Tej Singh was the only one we knew and he's locked up at the fort.'

'Hmm ... I suppose we'll find out. Well ... I'm in a hurry, I'll take my leave.'

Now how do I set him free, Chapla wondered, relieved to discover Tej's whereabouts. She sat down by the Ganga River and first ate some of the dried fruit she was carrying in her bag. Then she dressed up like a singing girl and made up her face so no one could recognize her. Finding a convenient spot behind the palace, she launched into a poignant love song. Her voice was naturally strong and resonant and she punctuated it with strains from a flute, heightening its effect.

The night was half spent. Maharaja Shivdutt was seated on the terrace with his queen when the sound of music reached his ears. The haunting notes stirred him so strongly that he became eager to find out who the singer was.

He sent for an attendant and said, 'Tell someone to call the person who's singing nearer the palace.'

The guards hurried to execute the king's order. For a moment Chapla's beauty struck them speechless. Then finding their voices, they said, 'His majesty has sent for you. He wants you to sing at a spot closer to the palace.'

Chapla rose and followed them. She launched into her song again, and the king was completely bewitched.

'Light up the main reception room!' he ordered. 'And escort the singer there.'

'Why can't she come here, inside the palace?' asked the queen.

'Let me first find out what kind of woman she is,' Shivdutt said.

He hurried to the hall. Chapla, who was already there, bent low and salaamed him. The king saw a woman of extraordinary beauty before him, dressed in a dark coloured sari tied in the Maharashtrian style, with one end tucked between her legs. She wore a bright green blouse, sprigged with flowers, and her loosely tied chignon was decorated with gold ornaments. Jewel-studded earrings hung from her ears, an intricately worked necklace clasped her neck and a golden tika adorned her forehead, while a girdle was looped around her slender waist. A closer look revealed a small black mole on her chin that enhanced her already overpowering looks. As if it were not enough, she had a perfectly formed figure.

'Come and sit here,' the king smiled, forgetting the queen.

Chapla stepped forward, her gait coy and inviting.

'Who are you?' Shivdutt asked, unable to take his eyes off her. 'What are you doing here, all alone in the middle of the night?'

'Maharaj, I come from Gwalior. My name is Rambha. My father was a well-known singer. I fell in love with a man but he left the city after a petty quarrel. I have been wandering through many royal courts hoping to find him, because he, too, is an accomplished singer. I was sitting there pouring my grief into a song, when your majesty sent for me.'

'You have an exceptional voice,' said the king. 'I wish to hear more.'

'I am deeply honoured,' Chapla bowed. 'But please send for your musicians. You'll enjoy my performance better then.'

The accompanists arrived, in a foul mood at being woken up at that hour. But when they set eyes on Chapla, they perked up and promptly tuned their instruments. And when she began to sing, everyone was transfixed, especially Shivdutt. After a couple of compositions in raag durbari, Chapla sang a bhairavi, then said, 'Maharaj, now that it's dawn, please grant me leave. I've travelled far and am very tired.'

The king looked around astonished. Lost in the music, he had not noticed the sun was about to rise. He removed a valuable pearl necklace from his neck and said, 'Stay here for a few days. I have not had enough of your singing.'

Chapla thanked him profusely. The king ordered that she be provided with a luxurious house to live in, along with servants to attend to her.

The same evening Shivdutt arranged for a public performance. Once again, Chapla held the audience in thrall.

After the first piece, she said, 'Your majesty, once I sang at the court of Naugarh. It was the most brilliant concert I have ever had. The reason was that the prime minister's son Tej Singh accompanied me on his *been*. I was there a few days back, but heard that he's disappeared.'

The king had surrendered his heart to Rambha. 'Well, he's my prisoner now,' he said, without thinking. 'I'm not going to set him free and he won't perform in captivity.'

'If he learns I'm here, he'll definitely agree,' Chapla said. 'Only, he's very stubborn. He will have to be summoned in a particular way.'

'And what's that?' asked the king.

'First, you must send a twenty-year-old Brahmin boy to fetch him, alone. You can shackle one of his legs for safety.

Then the pipe he's given to play should be of the best quality.'

Shivdutt found a boy called Chetram, who seemed suitable. He ordered an official to go and instruct the guards to let Tej accompany the boy. When Tej was summoned, he immediately guessed that it was a scheme cooked up by one of his friends, so he went willingly.

'Come, Tej Singh, Rambha has been waiting for a long time,' Chapla said loudly, when he entered the hall. 'Can I ever forget how well you played the *been* in Naugarh?' She winked swiftly.

Tej caught on at once. 'Oh, so it's you Rambha? Of course, I'll accompany you, even if I have to die in the process. Where would I ever find a singer like you?'

Shivdutt was surprised at this exchange. But he was so captivated with Chapla that he could not wait.

The recital began, and the audience listened enthralled. The king was lost to the world, in fact. However, after one song was over, Tej put the pipe down. 'I only play one piece a day. If you wish to hear more, I'll oblige you again tomorrow.'

'That's the problem with this fellow, your majesty,' Rambha frowned. 'Even Maharaja Surendra Singh couldn't persuade him.'

Shivdutt was astonished, wondering how this could benefit Tej. Anyway, he let him go. But he was so enamoured of Chapla that the next day he sent Chetram to fetch Tej again, and the two performed once more. Again Tej refused to play more than one piece. So the king gave orders that the performance should be repeated the next day.

The guards had got used to seeing Chetram come and fetch Tej. The following evening, an hour before the performance, Chapla arrived, dressed up as the boy. The guards let Tej go without a second thought and the two hurried from the palace. Once they were at a safe distance, Chapla removed the shackle on his foot and they plunged into the forest.

Chapla then took on her natural guise again.

'You are the cleverest girl I ever met!' Tej cried. 'No one else could have accomplished this.'

'Don't embarrass me,' Chapla said. 'I did what was required for Chandrakanta's sake.'

'Yes, why would you do it for me?' Tej replied. 'I'm the one who was eager to oblige you. I even acted as your accompanist, took on a task no one in my family ever dreamt of.'

'Please forgive me for putting you through that,' Chapla laughed.

'Just forgive you?' Tej said. 'You will have to pay me for it.'

'What do I have to give you?' Chapla asked.

'Whatever it is, it's sufficient for me.'

'Enough of this!' Chapla's brow furrowed purposefully. 'Do we plan to go back empty-handed or show Shivdutt a trick or two?'

'Spoken after my heart! What do you suggest?'

The two sat down and deliberated for a long time, then headed towards another dense forest.

*

Maharaja Shivdutt arrived at his reception hall all dressed up for the musical evening. When Rambha did not appear for some time, a soldier was sent to fetch her and Chetram to escort Tej.

The soldier came back with the report that she was not at home. Surprised, the king immediately ordered his men to go search for her. Then Chetram returned and reported that Tej Singh had escaped.

Shivdutt was stunned. The hall began to buzz with talk of the beautiful singer who had fooled everyone so cunningly. Ghasita and Chunnilal, who were present, said, 'Maharaj, this is definitely an aiyaar's doing.'

'True,' said Shivdutt, finding his voice, 'and that person deserves an award. Some extremely knowledgeable people were present and didn't suspect a thing. Perhaps they had lost their wits. You two don't deserve to be called aiyaars!'

He rose and swept into his chambers in a fury. The news spread through the town and everyone marvelled at this amazing piece of trickery.

When he arrived in court the next day, the king was still in a foul mood. He had barely begun the day's work, when a soldier appeared. 'Your majesty,' he said bowing, 'that singing girl was indeed a woman. She disguised herself as Chetram. I just saw her going into the Salai forest with Tej Singh.'

The king's face darkened. 'Go and capture them right away!' he ordered his soldiers.

'Your majesty,' the man said, bowing low, 'they might run away. If you send your aiyaars with me, I'll point them out from a distance. They can use their wiles to capture them.'

Shivdutt felt this was a good plan. The two aiyaars accompanied the soldier and he took them to the part of the forest where he said he had seen Tej Singh last.

'Now where are we to find them?' Ghasita said.

'Well it's not likely that they would have remained stuck here all this time,' said the man. 'You'll have to look for them.'

The three began to search. After a while, a milkmaid appeared, carrying pots of milk on her head. 'Did you see a man and a woman around here?' the soldier asked.

'Yes, deeper in the forest. In fact, I sold some milk to them.'

The soldier took out some money as a reward, but she refused saying, 'I don't take money for information. But if you wish to buy some milk, you're welcome to do so.'

'All right,' the man said.

The woman put her pots down. She poured out some milk. 'Won't you have some?' the soldier asked the aiyaars.

'We don't feel like it.' They shook their heads.

The soldier shrugged and gulped down the milk. 'Excellent!' he exclaimed, wiping his mouth. 'You won't get anything like this in the city.'

'Is that so?' Tempted, Chunnilal stretched out his hand for some. Ghasita followed suit.

They paid the woman and went ahead. Suddenly, the soldier stumbled. 'My head's whirling!' he cried.

'So's mine,' Ghasita said.

Chunnilal simply slumped to the ground.

The woman came running back. She revived the soldier

with smelling salts and Tej's face was revealed. The two tied up the aiyaars, hoisted them on their backs and hit the road leading to Naugarh.

Champa Proves her Mettle

When Chapla set off to rescue Tej, Champa realized she had to be extra careful. There were many aiyaars about and she was alone. She needed to be on guard constantly.

Therefore, she concocted a special powder. After Chandrakanta went to sleep, Champa made it into a paste and plastered it on the ground in front of the door. Then, feeling quite safe, she lay down beneath the princess's bed. This powder had a particular quality. It would make explosive sounds if anyone stepped on it.

The night passed without any incident, so she washed it off in the morning. The following night she moulded a head out of clay and painted it to look like Chandrakanta. She put this head on the princess's pillow with a dummy body and pulled up the covers. Then she spread the paste around the bed.

'Please sleep in another room tonight,' she said.

The princess smiled and retired to another chamber, while Champa occupied the room adjoining the dummy's.

Late at night, a loud bang startled her. Champa ran out and shut the door at once. She shouted for help and all the maids rushed there. 'Go tell his majesty that a thief has entered the princess's room!' she told them.

The guards were summoned and to Champa's delight, Pannalal and Ramnarayan were caught.

'You are a smart girl, indeed,' said the king, pleased to hear how efficiently Champa had guarded the princess. 'But where's Chapla?'

'Your majesty,' Champa said with downcast eyes, 'she's not feeling too well.'

'Oh . . . well, here's something for you.' He handed her a bag full of gold coins.

Champa bowed low and stepped back.

*

The two captives were produced in court the next day.

'What is your name?' Jai Singh asked Pannalal.

'Sartod Singh,' replied the man boldly.

This impertinence infuriated the king and he directed that they be kept under heavy guard. Later when he was alone with Hardayal, he asked, 'Have you any news of Tej Singh?'

'No, your majesty. If we beat these two soundly, perhaps they'll divulge something.'

'That is not permissible, according to their code. Tej will be upset,' Jai Singh said. 'Well, I'm sure he'll turn up. But we must keep our forces in readiness. Who knows when Shivdutt might choose to attack?'

But Shivdutt was preoccupied. After sending the two aiyaars to capture Tej Singh, he dismissed the court and returned to the palace. He had become so infatuated with Rambha that it was hard for him to concentrate on anything or even converse normally with his queen.

'What's the matter?' she asked. 'You look really pale.'

'Nothing. I stayed up too late last night,' he replied.

'There's something you've forgotten. You promised that you'd bring that singing girl to the palace to perform,' she said playfully.

'Don't talk about her!' the king groaned. 'She made a fool of all of us.'

'Oh . . . what did she do?'

'I'm not feeling so well right now,' Shivdutt looked away. 'I'll tell you later.'

He went and lay down in his private chamber. But thoughts of Rambha tormented him. Who *was* she? Why did she free Tej Singh? Was she in love with him? Oh, Rambha, what shall I do without you, he sighed.

Shivdutt spent a sleepless night. Next morning, when the

court assembled, he enquired, 'Have Ghasita and Chunnilal returned with any news?'

When he heard that there was no news of the aiyaars either, he was even more troubled. Rambha held his mind in thrall, even as he listened to all the petitions being presented before him. Later in the day, Badrinath, Nazim, Krur and the astrologer entered the court, salaamed him and sat down quietly. When he noticed their hangdog looks, his anxiety deepened. But he had to wait for the day's work to be completed before summoning them to speak to him in private.

'So, what did you accomplish in Vijaygarh?' he asked impatiently.

'Your majesty, you know I captured Tej Singh. But a girl named Champa snared Pannalal and Ramnarayan with great cunning. I managed to get away,' Badrinath said gloomily.

'And another woman managed to set Tej Singh free.' The king's mouth curled. 'Perhaps she has worsted Chunnilal and Ghasita Singh too. They went to search for the fugitives and haven't returned.' He glared at Krur. 'Helping you has proved disastrous for me . . . But first you people must find out who this woman is—who charmed me with her singing and fooled us. Her lovely face still haunts me.'

'Huzoor, I know who she is!' Nazim said at once. 'It has to be Chapla, Chandrakanta's companion.'

'Is she more beautiful than Chandrakanta?' asked the king.

'No, but if anyone is next to Chandrakanta in beauty, it is she,' Nazim said. 'And she is in love with Tej Singh.'

The king sat there stunned for a while, then clenched his fist. 'I cannot rest till I get hold of both those beauties. I'm going to write to Jai Singh.'

'But, Maharaj, he will not respond to your letter,' Krur said.

'Let him not. I'll wrest his kingdom from him and take them by force.'

He sent for his scribe and dictated a letter to Jai Singh asking for Chandrakanta's hand in marriage, adding that Chapla should be sent as part of her dowry.

Then he stamped his seal on it and asked Badrinath to deliver it. The aiyaar set off gleefully.

Good News and Bad

Maharaja Jai Singh sat in his court attending to his daily business, but thoughts of Tej Singh preoccupied him.

'Is there no news still?' he asked Hardayal.

The minister was about to reply, when a man entered the court bent under a huge load.

'There he is!' Hardayal beamed.

Tej Singh plonked the bundle right in the middle of the court, creating a buzz of astonishment. He salaamed the king, who motioned to him to sit down.

'So, where have you been all these days?' Jai Singh asked. 'We have been searching for you frantically. Your father must be very worried. We sent someone to enquire there too.'

'Your majesty, your servant was snared by the enemy,' Tej

replied. 'But by the grace of your blessings I was set free and managed to bring two aiyaars from Chunar as well.'

'Superbly done!' The king removed a valuable bracelet from his wrist. Tej bowed and accepted it. Jai Singh added, 'Champa captured two more, here in the palace. Let these fellows be sent to the same prison.'

The guards opened the bundle and took the aiyaars away.

'Maharaj,' Tej said, 'if you permit, I'll go visit my family at Naugarh and relieve their anxiety.'

'Of course, you must,' the king nodded. 'But please return as soon as possible. Hardayal, kindly accompany him and carry plenty of gifts.'

*

Overjoyed to have her friend back, Chandrakanta embraced Chapla joyfully.

'Tell me what happened, quickly!' she asked. 'I can't wait. And don't you dare leave anything out!'

Chapla smiled. She hugged Champa too, then took a seat and launched into the tale of her escapades.

'What amazing exploits!' The princess squeezed Chapla's hand hard when she had finished. 'Thank God, you returned safely. Your disciple acquitted herself well too. She put two aiyaars to shame.'

'Is that so?' Chapla clasped Champa close again.

*

Tej and Hardayal Singh arrived at Maharaja Surendra Singh's court the next morning.

The moment Virendra saw him, he jumped up, as excited as if he'd found a treasure.

Tej prostrated himself before the king and touched his father's feet. Hardayal greeted them too and presented the gifts. Among them was a set of clothes for Virendra.

'You must put them on right away,' Tej said. The prince went off to do so joyfully.

'They certainly suit you,' said the king, when he reappeared. 'Or is it your smile that's brightening up the brocade coat?'

There was a burst of laughter from the courtiers. 'But Tej,' the king's face sobered as he continued, 'what happened to you?'

'Ah, your majesty,' Tej said, hanging his head, 'I'm afraid I was outmanoeuvred. I gave it back to them though, in full measure. I tricked the guards and escaped Maharaja Shivdutt's prison and even captured two of his aiyaars.'

'Well done,' said the king, 'but your mother must be waiting for you. Go and meet her. She'll be relieved to see that you've come back unhurt.'

While Surendra Singh was entertaining Hardayal, the prince slipped away to his chambers. He was eager to talk to Tej in private. Tej was as keen to share the real account of his escape, which he had kept from the rest of the company, for the sake of Chapla's honour. He tore himself away from his mother, promising to be back soon, and hurried to meet his friend.

'You're squeezing the breath out of me!' he laughed as the prince enveloped him in a bear hug.

'Oh, Tej, you can't imagine how anxious I've been,' Virendra replied. 'I know what a scoundrel Shivdutt is.'

'That he is,' Tej nodded. Then he smiled mischievously. 'But there's a girl who can worst such scoundrels with her bare left hand.'

'Who is she?' the prince asked, frowning. 'We must get her on our side.'

'It will not be easy,' Tej said with a twinkle in his eye. Then he burst out laughing. 'It was none other than our dear Chapla, who used her wiles to set me free!'

'Chapla!' The prince's eyes almost popped out with astonishment. 'Amazing! But how did she manage that?'

Tej told him how Chapla had hatched a brilliant scheme to set him free.

'What devotion! What courage! What cunning!' the prince was thunderstruck. 'I congratulate you, my dear friend.'

'I will congratulate you first.' Tej thumped the prince's back. 'Then only will my turn come!'

The prince flushed scarlet as Tej doubled up with laughter.

Several enjoyable days went by, full of such pleasantries and good cheer. Then Hardayal Singh said to the king, 'Your majesty, your hospitality cannot be measured in words. But I have to return to my duties. And if you would permit, Maharaja Jai Singh has requested that Tej go back with me.'

Surendra Singh readily agreed, and the two took leave.

The prince's face was dark with gloom, however.

'Don't look so dejected,' Tej said. 'Your troubles will soon be over, I promise!'

*

Hardayal and Tej had just arrived at Vijaygarh and were paying their respects to Jai Singh, when Shivdutt's messenger entered.

Badrinath respectfully offered the letter to Jai Singh and the king handed it to Hardayal to read, as was the custom. Hardayal's face flamed as he went through it. Both the king and Tej, who were watching, guessed at once that the contents were disrespectful.

Hardayal finished the letter and turned to the monarch. In a voice trembling with outrage, he said, 'Your majesty, I would like to read this to you in private.'

The king nodded. 'Kindly make arrangements for Badrinath's stay,' he said. 'Then I'll see you and Tej at my private chambers.'

When they arrived, Hardayal handed the letter to Jai Singh and said, 'It is better that you read it yourself, your majesty.'

Within seconds Jai Singh's eyes were blazing. He tore the letter into bits and flung it on the ground.

'Tell the messenger,' he said, grinding his teeth, 'the answer is that he leave this place immediately.'

The distraught king was silent for a while. Then he added,

'I knew Krur would not rest till he had stirred up trouble for me. But I will not allow his nefarious designs to succeed while I live. We must prepare for battle.'

'Yes. Shivdutt will definitely arrive with his army soon,' Tej said. 'We cannot lose time.'

'He may have a force of thirty thousand men,' Jai Singh's nostrils flared, 'but does he think that will scare me? Our ten thousand will be more than a match.'

'Indeed, your majesty,' Tej said. 'You can add five thousand more from Naugarh and we'll rout that army of jackals with ease. If you would send Hardayalji with a letter, Prince Virendra will get his troops ready at once. And if you leave everything to him, you'll see how he trounces Shivdutt.'

The minister had misgivings, but Tej said, 'Both Maharaja Surendra Singh and Virendra are courageous warriors. They will never sit back and watch others fight. Believe me!'

Hardayal was sent post-haste with a letter to the Naugarh court. The news created a furore there too.

After the initial shock, Virendra sprang into action. 'If you permit, sir,' he said to his father, 'I'll take an army to Chunar right away. I'll seize that scoundrel Shivdutt before he can set foot on the Vijaygarh road.'

'There's no need to be in such a hurry. Go to Vijaygarh first,' said the king. 'As a kshatriya I consider it more honourable to fight a noble war, than be concerned about the safety of my flesh and blood. Therefore, setting my fatherly feelings aside, I'm ordering you to go to Jai Singh's aid!'

The troops were instructed to get ready overnight so they could leave for Vijaygarh the next morning.

The prospect of meeting Chandrakanta and fighting for her was so enchanting that the prince felt the night speed by in a flash. The moment dawn broke, he bathed and arrayed himself in his battle dress, and armed himself with all his weapons.

'Go with my blessings, son,' said his mother, as he took leave of her. 'And do us proud.'

Virendra mounted his horse and took the lead, along with Hardayal Singh. The army followed him, looking like waves rolling across a sea.

As they approached Vijaygarh, the prince said, 'Perhaps I should stop here in the forest and settle my soldiers, while you go and inform his majesty.'

Hardayal agreed and went to notify the king. Overjoyed, Jai Singh instructed the minister to go with the commanders of his army and escort the prince to the court with due honour.

Tej heard everything and headed for the forest immediately. 'Hearty congratulations!' he shouted, the moment he saw the prince. 'It's all working out the way we wished! And will continue to do so, I know.'

He plunged into the task of setting up camp for the soldiers. Soon Hardayal arrived with the officers and conveyed Jai Singh's invitation.

Word that Prince Virendra Singh had come to Jai Singh's aid with his army spread through the city like wildfire. The people spilled on to the streets to greet them. Hordes climbed their roofs to get a good view.

When the news of their approach reached the royal household, a band of women hurried up to the terrace of the palace to gaze at the spectacle. Chandrakanta and Chapla were among them. The king could not contain himself either and ascended the roof of his reception room.

First, a cloud of dust appeared to the north of the city. Then little by little, the procession came into view. It was indeed magnificent. The rays of the setting sun lit up the men's armour, and the sight of their flags and spears, the swords hanging at their waists, the shields on their backs, greatly stirred the hearts of the spectators.

Virendra Singh led them, mounted on a splendid horse. Decorated with a jewelled harness and saddle, it pranced along playfully. The sun's heat added a warm flush to the prince's face, his large eyes gleamed with enthusiasm. The string of striking emeralds he wore on his neck, along with a matching armlet, added their glow. His waistband was studded with an imposing diamond surrounded by other precious stones, and his knee-length boots were embroidered so densely with pearls that not a millimetre of leather could be glimpsed. Armed with a sword, shield, dagger, bow and arrow, with a spear in his hand, he was a majestic sight. More so, the zest for battle that suffused his handsome face roused admiration in the hearts of his friends, even while it alarmed his enemies. A hundred horsemen accompanied him, almost as impressive.

The queen had not seen Virendra for a long time. The moment she set eyes on him, she exclaimed, 'If there's anyone worthy of our dear Chandrakanta, it is Virendra. Come what may, he will be my son-in-law.'

Chapla cast a sidelong glance at the princess, who flushed a deep red. Her heart had already taken wing. The prince's image imprinted itself in her eyes and she thrilled with the hope of meeting him.

Even the king could not take his eyes off the fine-looking prince. When he approached the gates of the fort, Jai Singh hurried to greet him. Virendra bent to touch his feet. The king embraced him and led him to the palace. The queen welcomed him affectionately, but Virendra's eyes were searching the group of richly clad girls around her for Chandrakanta. He little knew that she was watching him, hidden behind a door. She longed to meet him, but dared not express her desire openly. After the courtesies were over, the prince was escorted to a lavishly furnished apartment. Tej arrived and they chatted for some time. But Virendra was restless and downcast, because he had not been able to see his beloved. He dozed off on the luxurious bed, wondering how he could.

The next morning, he rose and attired himself in the silk and brocades of his formal court dress, put a jewelled ornament in his turban and presented himself before Jai Singh.

'Here's the letter from his majesty Surendra Singh of Naugarh,' Hardayal said, handing over the missive.

Jai Singh's eyes sped through it and his face lit up. 'Kindly send provisions for the Naugarh forces immediately,' he said. 'They must not lack for anything.'

The prince instructed Tej to divide his troops into three parts and spread them around Vijaygarh. 'Send out spies in all four directions,' he said. 'We'll decide how to deploy his majesty's army tomorrow.'

Within minutes, messengers began to speed to and fro.

The lines of anxiety had already begun to smooth themselves out from Jai Singh's face, when some spies hurried up. 'Your majesty,' one said, 'we have learnt that Shivdutt has left Chunar with a thirty-thousand strong army. They are likely to arrive here within two-three days.'

'Never mind, we'll take care of them,' the prince said, confidently. 'Go and attend to your duties. Would you like to inspect the troops, your majesty?'

Jai Singh nodded his assent and the two set off. When both were satisfied with the arrangements, the prince said, 'Your majesty, our defences seem to be in place. If you permit, I'd like to spend the afternoon hunting.'

'Certainly,' said the king. 'But don't go too far and please return before nightfall.'

He sent an escort of a hundred men with the prince.

The truth was that Virendra was longing to meet Chandrakanta but did not know how to accomplish it. He hoped this excursion would act as a diversion.

The Enemy Strikes

The party rode into the forest and soon the prince downed a deer with his arrows. As he went deeper into the bushes to recover his prey, Tej suddenly appeared.

'How are the arrangements going?' the prince asked.

'Everything will be set by tomorrow,' Tej replied. 'I wanted to go to the grotto and check out the prisoners. Would you like to come?'

'Why not?' Virendra said. He told his escort to pick up the fallen deer and take it back to the city.

When they reached the prison door, Tej asked, 'Do you remember how to open this?'

'Of course,' Virendra replied. 'It doesn't need any great artistry.' He pulled out the lion's tongue, the door opened and they found Ahmed and Bhagwandutt deep in conversation.

'Won't your highness let us go now?' the two asked, salaaming deeply.

'You have to stay here a few days longer,' the prince replied.

Then he and Tej locked the door and headed towards the city. When they were close, Tej said, 'I'll go inspect the arrangements again.'

Virendra nodded and returned to his quarters. He was quite exhausted, so he rested for a while.

Later that night Tej reappeared. 'What a hectic day!' he said. 'I've managed to complete everything as we had planned. But I couldn't get away and meet you for even an hour.'

'You couldn't find time to meet me!' Virendra laughed, 'What about all the time we spent together this afternoon?'

'What do you mean?' Tej started up. 'I met you?'

'Didn't you come with me to the cave prison to check on the aiyaars?'

Tej paled. He stared at the prince wide-eyed. Baffled, Virendra narrated the afternoon's events.

'You've ruined everything!' Tej clutched his forehead. 'I don't care much that they got away. But they've learnt how to unlock the secret door. That's a serious matter!'

'I don't understand. What are you talking about?'

'If you had that much understanding you wouldn't have fallen into their trap,' Tej replied. 'Shivdutt's aiyaars made a fool of you. Well, I'd better go and repair the damage right away.'

'What?' Virendra looked stricken. 'But … what will you do now?'

'Luckily there are other better ways of locking the door. They were too complicated, that's why I didn't use them earlier.'

Tej hurried away.

*

The sun was already up when he returned next morning.

'The birds have flown but I've changed the lock,' he told the anxious Virendra.

Quickly they got ready to attend court. Barely had they arrived when a spy rushed in. 'Your majesty, Shivdutt's forces are just twenty miles away!' he announced breathlessly.

'It's time to send the frontline troops in, your majesty,' Virendra said.

'Please do it immediately,' Jai Singh said.

Tej sprang up and set off with Hardayal. The prince stayed back with the king. Thoughts of Chandrakanta tormented him, but he did not dare ask her father if he could meet her. However, she had her fill of gazing at him, unobserved. And thus the day passed.

That night, as Virendra was discussing strategy for the forthcoming battle with the king, Tej and Hardayal, some guards burst in.

'Your majesty, a band of intruders just ran out of the

Chormahal! The sentries shot and wounded a few with their arrows. But they managed to escape.'

They had barely finished speaking when the sound of shrieking and wailing came to their ears. It grew louder and louder and the king and Virendra both sprang up, alarmed. But before they could act, a group of maids dashed in. Tears were pouring down their faces.

'Someone broke in and . . . and cut off Chandrakanta's and Chapla's heads!' they cried out together, controlling their sobs with great difficulty.

These terrible words struck Virendra dumb with grief. His face turned ashen and no sound emerged from his lips.

The king cried out, 'Hai!' and fell down unconscious.

Tej remained rooted to his seat, stiff as a wooden image. But Hardayal could not hold back his tears. After a while, the king came back to his senses. Weeping uncontrollably, he caught hold of Virendra's hand. The others collected themselves and headed for the women's wing of the palace.

The scene was horrible beyond description. The whole room was spattered with blood. The headless bodies of the princess and her companion lay on the floor, a ghastly sight. The queen sat bent over Chandrakanta's corpse frantically beating her breast. Overcome, the king fell on the body and wept like a child while Virendra simply collapsed by the door.

When Tej saw Virendra lying there, as bloodless as a corpse, he turned to stone. Pulling out his dagger, he cried, 'If you have gone, my beloved friend, I have no desire to live either!'

That very moment, a man leapt through the door. He

was covered all over with orange sindoor powder.

'Why fling your precious life away
Listen first to what I have to say
It's nothing but a game of tricks
Arise, arise and know the corpse!'

He bared all his teeth in a grimace and leaping and prancing, left as suddenly as he had come.

The whole group gazed at him stunned. Then Tej struck his forehead. 'He's right!' he cried out. 'It's an aiyaar's trick. These are dummies.'

The queen dried her tears and turned to Tej. 'You mean Chandrakanta's alive? But whose bodies are these?'

Tej shook his head. 'I don't know. But it looks as if Shivdutt's aiyaars have abducted Chandrakanta and Chapla and left these dummies to confuse us.'

The king looked unconvinced, so taking out his knife, Tej cut off the leg from one of the bodies.

'You are right,' Jai Singh said. 'There's no bone in it. Thank God, my daughter lives! But she's fallen into the hands of the enemy. And that's almost as bad.'

'Don't worry, your majesty,' Tej said. 'Come what may, I'll rescue them. But our prince still lies unconscious.'

Virendra was carried to his room. Tej closed the doors and whispered in his ear, 'Chandrakanta is alive! She has to be rescued from Shivdutt. What kind of gallantry is this—to lie lifeless and do nothing?'

The prince blinked. Then sat up agitated and said, 'Who says the enemy has abducted Chandrakanta? You, Tej? How do you know?'

'Examine the bodies,' Tej challenged.

Virendra looked at them carefully, then embraced his friend too overcome to speak. The two got busy discussing strategies to free the two girls with Jai Singh. Dawn was beginning to break when Hardayal entered.

He salaamed deeply and said, 'Maharaj, I heard about the dummy corpses. I cannot describe my relief. However, another problem has cropped up. While the guards were all running around in a state of shock, Shivdutt's aiyaars attacked the few who remained on duty and freed their companions.'

'This is a serious setback!' the prince cried out. 'They've got all their aiyaars back. We must attack at once.'

The words were barely out of his mouth when a spy was ushered in. 'Sire,' he said, 'our frontline troops fought bravely and massacred a thousand of the enemy. However, they are badly outnumbered and need support immediately.'

The prince got to his feet and said, 'Hardayalji, please order that five thousand men be sent to relieve them. I will lead them myself. This is a good opportunity to test Shivdutt's valour.' He turned to Jai Singh. 'You need not trouble yourself right now, your majesty. Please attend to your affairs here.'

By late afternoon the camp had been set up. Hundreds of tents stretched out in a semi-circular formation towards the east. Virendra's men got busy cleaning their weapons.

Cannons had been placed beneath large canopies. The horses were stabled in the south with the elephants tethered close by. The air resounded with their trumpeting, which mingled with the whinnying of the horses. The drummers, dynamiters and spies had their camps on the west, next to the provision store.

The prince was deep in discussion, planning the attack with Tej and Fateh Singh the commander-in-chief, when they caught sight of Devi Singh approaching them. Both Tej and the prince embraced him joyfully. Tej informed the others that he was the mysterious man who had first warned them about the king's approach when the prince had secretly visited Chandrakanta's garden. He had also told them that Krur was returning with the Chunar aiyaars and, finally, that he was the one who revealed that the two bodies were actually dummies.

'Where do you think Chandrakanta could be?' Virendra asked.

'Right now, all I know is that Nazim and Badrinath carried her and Chapla away,' he replied.

'This is a pretty pickle,' Tej frowned. 'We are outnumbered nine to two. I don't know whether I should go and rescue the ladies or protect the prince.'

'We should deal with Shivdutt first, then everything will fall into place,' Devi Singh said.

The idea appealed to all of them.

The Battle

The following morning, after the forces were ready and beginning to march towards the battlefield, Devi was sent to Shivdutt's camp with the following letter:

'It seems that you have deliberately decided to antagonize Maharaja Jai Singh. Kindly return Chandrakanta and Chapla, whom your aiyaars abducted. Act like an honourable man, else our warriors will give you no quarter.'

Devi approached the enemy camp boldly. Arrogant as ever, Shivdutt sat on a golden throne inside a luxuriously furnished tent, surrounded by his officers and aiyaars. Devi placed the letter on the throne, without greeting anyone.

The king snatched up the letter, read it and tore it into bits. 'The mosquito thinks he can do battle with a lion.' He curled his lip contemptuously. 'Capture this impudent fellow!'

Devi immediately drew his dagger, making short shrift of the guards who leapt at him. Then he pulled out a ball-like object from his bag and flung it on the ground. It exploded so loudly that everyone jumped. Shivdutt's turban fell off his head, along with its diamond ornament. Devi grabbed it and fled.

There was much merriment in Virendra's camp when Devi returned and narrated the incident. Tej promptly removed the ornament from the turban and put it into his bag.

'Why did you do that?' asked the prince.

'The day you get married I'll dress up like Shivdutt and lead the procession with this ornament of victory in my turban,' Tej replied.

The prince laughed, though soon after a couple of tears dropped from his eyes.

'You stay here with the prince, Devi, while I go and look for Chandrakanta and Chapla,' Tej said. 'I know the hills of Chunar better than you. And please take good care of yourself, my friend.'

It had turned dark now. Tej lost no time getting ready. Soon he had disappeared in the dense forest.

However, Virendra's anxiety could not be assuaged. He tossed and turned all night, haunted by thoughts of Chandrakanta's plight. When the first streaks of light appeared, war drums resounded from Shivdutt's camp. Eagerly, he rose and donned his battle gear.

Both armies were massed on the plain. Virendra galloped up on his Arab steed and beckoned to Devi. 'We should tell Shivdutt that the blood of innocent soldiers should not be shed in a personal battle. If he considers himself as brave as Arjun, I'm prepared for a man to man fight.'

'You are right,' Devi said. 'I'll see to it right away.'

He hurried to the field and tossed his shoulder cloth three times in the air. Immediately Badrinath appeared from the other side and said, 'Jai Maya! Why do you summon the aiyaars?'

'Jai Maya!' Devi replied. 'I just wanted to ask if you have any fearless warriors on your side.'

'We have many such men,' Badrinath said arrogantly.

'Why do you wish to slaughter the poor soldiers then? If Maharaja Shivdutt has the stomach for it, our prince would be too happy to fight him man to man. And let whoever wins rule Chunar.'

'Our king will squash your prince between his fingers,' Badrinath sneered.

'So let him come into the field!' Devi replied.

Badrinath carried the message back to Shivdutt. It was like a red rag to a bull. The king sprang on to his horse and charged on to the field, shaking his spear menacingly.

Virendra spurred his horse on too and faced Shivdutt. 'Do valiant men steal innocent girls?' he shouted. 'If you were truly courageous you would have fought for Chandrakanta's hand and won her on the battlefield.'

Infuriated, Shivdutt flung his spear at Virendra, who

struck it away with his own so violently that both flew through the air and fell far off. Impressed, even Shivdutt's troops cheered the prince. This maddened the king further. He pulled out his sword and dashed at Virendra. The prince parried his strokes expertly. The duel continued back and forth till the sun hung low in the sky. Finally a blow from Virendra's sword wounded Shivdutt's horse. It slumped to the ground. The king had incurred many injuries too. He abandoned his horse and attacked Virendra's. But the prince struck Shivdutt's wrist with his whip and the sword fell from his hand.

Seeing that the fight was going against him, Shivdutt signalled to his men. Within minutes, the enemy surrounded Virendra. But Fateh Singh and Devi joined the fray, striking out with sword and dagger. The prince fought so bravely that he wreaked havoc amongst Shivdutt's greatest warriors. Then dusk began to fall and the drums sounded, signalling the end of battle for the day.

Shivdutt's leaders took stock. They had thought it would be child's play to destroy Virendra's small army. Instead they had been hard pressed by their doughty foes. In desperation they decided to launch a surprise attack by night.

Shivdutt struck in the late hours with a force of five hundred. Taken by surprise, Virendra's men could not make out friend from foe in the dark and injured many of their own people by mistake.

Virendra promptly arranged for torches to be lit. Once the troops could see clearly, they decimated the attacking force with ease. But a large number of the prince's men had been killed. Despite his distress, Virendra was still fighting when dawn broke.

Suddenly, a troop of warriors galloped up from the northeast. A well-dressed man riding an Arab steed led them. They charged full pelt into the battle. This leader was masked, as were the five hundred troops who lit into Shivdutt's army from the rear. Heartened by this support, Virendra's forces perked up and fought with renewed vigour. Shivdutt's soldiers could not withstand the two-pronged attack and took to their heels. Virendra chased the fleeing enemy for a couple of miles. When they did not stop and fight back, he signalled for the drums of victory to be beaten. To his surprise, the mysterious soldiers rode off in the same direction from which they had come.

Virendra gazed after them, confused. Who were these anonymous supporters who would not wait to be thanked?

Shivdutt's belongings fell into the hands of the victorious army. The prince started to relax. But soon a spy informed him that the enemy had halted some distance away and was regrouping for battle.

The Search

Tej had to figure out first where Chandrakanta was confined. It seemed likely that the aiyaars would have taken her to Chunar, so he headed there. But an extensive search of the city did not provide any clues. So that night, when he found an unguarded spot, he crept into the fort, disguised. Covering himself with a black cloth, he flung his rope over the palace walls and climbed up. It was close to midnight and the place was deathly still. As he prowled the courtyard, he glimpsed light in one room. When he peeped in, he found a few dim lamps illuminating a chamber furnished with costly hangings and beautiful pictures. Some women were sleeping on the floor while one lay alone on a high mattress.

Tej tiptoed in and put out all the lamps save one. He looked at the woman closely. She made a lovely picture as she slept and he guessed she must be Shivdutt's queen. He took out pen and paper from his bag and quickly wrote a note. Then he placed a powder beneath the queen's nose. She inhaled it and fell unconscious. Tej tucked the note under her pillow, picked her up and carried her out through a window that overlooked the Ganga.

He swiftly made for the hills. After administering another dose of the knock-out powder, he concealed the queen in a ravine. Then he returned to the fort and hid by the gate.

*

When dawn broke, the maids discovered the queen missing. Alarmed, they ran through the fort searching for her. In the meantime, the defeated Shivdutt arrived with a few horsemen. He got the bad news at the gate and rushed inside to find pandemonium. Overcome, he slumped down by the queen's bed with his face in his hands. He had returned to Chunar just to check up on matters here, leaving his aiyaars behind with some troops to prepare for further battle.

Suddenly, he noticed a piece of paper sticking out from beneath her pillow. When he read it, he was even more perplexed: 'I don't know why, but I feel like meeting Chandrakanta. I know where she is staying and am going there.'

It was not the queen's handwriting. And even if she had

written it, how had she found out where Chandrakanta was confined? Shivdutt's confusion escalated. His aiyaars were not around. If he asked anyone else to investigate, the story would be out. Many of his men were already searching for the queen. After much thought, he decided to go and find out for himself, but later.

When dusk fell, Shivdutt sent for a horse and left the fort all alone. It was a moonlit night and Tej, who was still sitting by the gate, recognized him immediately. He followed the king stealthily. After going about six miles, the king turned his horse into the dry bed of a stream. The gully deepened as they progressed, and the tall trees whose branches met overhead gave it a tunnel-like appearance. Finally, there was a glimmer of light and Tej noticed that they were close to a small cave. At least twenty heavily built men stood on guard, carrying naked swords. The inside of the cave was clearly visible. Tej caught sight of two women seated on a wide rock.

They were Chandrakanta and Chapla.

The guards helped the king off his horse and lit torches. Now Tej got a better look at the girls. Chandrakanta looked pale, her hair was dishevelled. He even noticed a gash on her head. Covered with dust, she reclined against a rock, dazed. Chapla sat near her, cradling the princess's head in her hand. Food lay before them, untouched. They both looked so demoralized and hopeless that tears stung Tej's eyes.

Shivdutt searched the place thoroughly. Finding nothing, he strode out and mounted his horse, without a word to anyone or even a glance at Chandrakanta. Tej hurriedly retreated—the gully was too narrow for him to hide.

Shivdutt set off towards the city, but Tej was in a quandary. He could not overpower the guards by himself. Neither could he disguise himself as the king because he had just been there. He had to act cautiously, lest Chandrakanta be moved to another place. He decided to return to Vijaygarh and come back with help.

He reached there the next afternoon. The prince rose and embraced him. 'Is there any news?' he asked eagerly.

'Yes,' Tej replied.

Virendra's face lit up and he immediately dismissed his retinue. Only Fateh Singh and Devi remained. Tej told them what he had discovered. 'I didn't want to take any chances,' he said, 'or do anything that might cause injury to the princess. I've come to take Devi with me. Now that Shivdutt has been vanquished you don't need him.'

'I'll come along too,' said the prince. 'There is no likelihood of battle now and Fateh Singh is here to keep an eye on things.'

The three set off. The path was clearly visible in the moonlight and they must have gone about eight miles when they caught sight of Badrinath. He salaamed the prince politely.

Virendra laughed in reply, and Devi said, 'Badrinathji, why do you keep company with cowards and thieves? Join our court and you'll discover what honour and justice truly mean.'

'That may be right,' the aiyaar replied. 'But I cannot think of it till this matter of Maharaja Shivdutt's is resolved. Would you trust me if I switched sides now?'

He turned away and disappeared in the forest.

'This is not good,' Tej said. 'Now he'll try to find out where we are going.'

'Yes, an ill omen indeed,' Devi sighed.

'What should we do now?' asked the prince.

'Nothing much, except take the open path through the plain. If anyone tries to follow us, we'll spot them right away,' Tej said.

They left the forest and travelled through the plain, keeping constant watch lest anyone was on their trail. When day broke, they washed at a stream. By noon they had reached the ravine where Chandrakanta was confined.

'This is a job best done by night,' Tej said. 'We might as well rest under this tree.'

They spread out a tarpaulin and tethered the prince's horse with a long rope and let it graze. When the sun set, they entered the gully, after looking around carefully to see if anyone was observing them. However, when they approached the cave, Tej was mystified to find the place in darkness.

When they came to the door, Tej lit a flare. All three froze at the sight before them. The lifeless bodies of the guards lay on the earth. Worse, Chandrakanta and Chapla could not be found! Only broken bits of their ornaments remained and blood spattered all over.

'She's gone! She's gone forever!' Virendra's dagger clattered to the ground.

'Why do you lose heart?' Tej said. 'If they had killed her, her body would be lying here.'

'Do you think Badrinath is involved?' Devi asked.

'But why would they slaughter their own men?' Tej frowned. 'Well, we'll find out soon.'

Somehow they managed to persuade the downcast prince to get moving. 'Let's check the place where you confined the queen,' Devi said.

However, when they got there, they found the queen missing too! For a while, they just sat there confounded, disheartened.

Then Devi said, 'I've got an idea, guruji. You relax here, I'll try and find out what's going on.'

He made for Chunar, which was not too far. Disguising himself as a rustic brahmin, he approached a soldier on guard at the palace. 'Sir,' he said, showing him a bottle, 'can you identify this attar? A man said he'd give me five silver coins if I could. But I'm a simple villager and don't know about these things. Perhaps *you* do, being attached to the palace. I'll give you one coin if you can help me.'

Tempted by the reward, the soldier sniffed the bottle deeply and fell unconscious. Devi bundled him up and carried him back.

When he came to, Tej asked the bewildered man, 'Tell us where your queen is?'

The man remained silent. But after he received a kick from Tej, he said, 'She's been missing for several days. That's all I know.'

Tej tied the man to a tree and took the prince aside. 'It would be better if you returned to the camp. It'll take several days to solve this mystery. If Shivdutt learns you're not there, he might attack again.'

'No. I'll stay here. I don't care what happens,' the prince replied.

It took a lot of convincing to make him agree to return the next day, if they were unable to find Chandrakanta. Then Tej disguised himself as the soldier they had captured and went off to Chunar.

Virendra and Devi spent the night in the forest. This portion was so dense that no one could approach it easily. Dawn was about to break, when a small stone landed near the prince. Astonished, the two were gazing at it, when another fell even closer to them.

'Who's throwing stones?' Devi shouted. 'Why don't you come out and face us?'

'Jackals who try to roar like lions have to be treated this way!' someone replied.

Infuriated, the prince sprang up, hand on his sword. Devi grabbed his arm. 'Why do you bother?' he said. 'I'll go catch the rascal.'

He dashed towards the spot where the voice seemed to be coming from. Another stone landed in his path. Devi caught a glimpse of a man, but could not see his face clearly. The dense vegetation blocked the light. He gave swift chase. The man threw another stone, then zigzagged among the trees like a fox and vanished completely. The aiyaar continued to hunt for him till the sun was well above his head, then gave up in disgust. When he returned to the spot where he had left the prince, his heart sank with dismay.

Both Virendra and the captive had gone!

*

Tej arrived at the gate of the fort, disguised. The other guards called out, 'Where did you vanish, Jairam Singh? Badrinath came to check and was furious. He's gone to look for you.'

Tej said, 'My stomach was upset. I went to relieve myself and found I had severe diarrhoea. Oh, I need to go again!'

He hurried off, knowing that if Badrinath came back, he would be exposed. He dressed up like a beggar and sat by the road awaiting the aiyaar's return. Soon his patience was rewarded. Badrinath arrived with Nazim behind him, carrying a bundle on his back. And behind Nazim was the guard Jairam Singh.

The smug look on Badrinath's face disturbed Tej. He knew what this meant. The bundle had to contain either the prince or Devi Singh. After the three entered the fort, he made for the forest at full speed. He found Devi sitting there morosely.

'Guruji,' he cried, falling at Tej's feet, 'the prince has fallen into the hands of the enemy!' He told Tej what had happened.

'What terrible times!' Tej shook his head. 'As if it weren't enough that Chandrakanta and Chapla have been abducted! But we have to find a way out of this mess somehow.'

For a while they sat there discussing possible plans , then set off together.

Captive!

In a small room inside Shivdutt's palace, Virendra lay slumped dejectedly. His hands and feet were fettered. The windows were barred and female guards walked up and down outside, with daggers at their waists.

The prince's face was ashen. 'Even if they find Chandrakanta what can *I* do? I don't mind being shut up . . . if I could only be sure that she was safe and well,' he muttered to himself. 'Ah . . . if I was roaming the forest searching for her, I wouldn't mind starving, being slashed by the sharpest thorns. Dear God, why was she born a princess, if she was fated to suffer like this?'

Tears kept flowing from his eyes. It was well past midnight, but sleep had abandoned him.

A lavishly decorated courtyard lay right before this chamber illuminated by four or five lamps, even at this hour. Suddenly the prince noticed maids bringing more lights. Within minutes the place was so brightly lit that it seemed like day. After spreading a silken mattress on the ground, the maids stood there, as if waiting for someone. The prince watched, with puckered brows. He was a little surprised that Shivdutt had confined him in the women's palace where even the scent of a strange man was forbidden.

He saw Shivdutt arrive, dressed in the richest robes. And then a current jerked through his frame. He stared as if he could not believe his eyes. Two women were seating themselves on the mattress next to the king—on his right and left. Chandrakanta and Chapla!

More astonishing, they sat close to Shivdutt, touching him. Chandrakanta's beauty dazzled Virendra. Today she looked lovely beyond compare. Containers holding paan, bottles of perfume and other such dainties lay nearby.

The prince's eyes reddened with an uncontrollable rage. Had Chandrakanta willingly surrendered herself to Shivdutt? Had she forgotten her love for him? Even her devotion to her parents? Didn't she know that he languished there, a helpless prisoner, right in front of her? And what had happened to Chapla, who had risked her life to set Tej free from this very king? Had her affections too shifted to Shivdutt? Look at the way she reclined against him! Alas, who could fathom a woman's heart! It was utterly foolish to trust one. Why had fate ordained that he fall in love with such a fickle girl? And who could imagine that a high-born princess could behave this way? I have nothing to live for now, he thought, but I'll see to it that Shivdutt cannot enjoy them either. True, brave men do not lay their hands on women, but I don't care for such niceties now. If Tej were here, he too would support me.

Just then, Chandrakanta coyly put an arm around Shivdutt's neck. This action pushed Virendra to the very edge. He tore off his handcuffs and kicked the barred door down. One swift leap carried him to Shivdutt. He picked up the sword that lay near the king and with one powerful stroke, slashed Chandrakanta's head from her body. Before Shivdutt could react, Chapla met the same fate.

The king stood there dumbfounded, all his valour evaporated.

And as Virendra loomed over him with the naked, bloodstained sword in his hand, Tej and Devi leapt into the room.

'Well done!' Tej Singh cried. In one swift movement he flung the rope around Shivdutt's neck. The king fell to the ground, Devi bundled him up.

'Hurry,' Tej said. 'Don't speak. I know what you're going through.'

No one tried to stop them. The few maids that were there were too stunned to do anything.

A Ray of Hope

The prince followed the aiyaars like a puppet. He did not speak or question them. He seemed removed from this world. He did not care where he was being taken or what was happening around him. When they had gone deep into the forest, Devi set down the bundle he was carrying. Tej dusted a rock with his shoulder cloth and asked the prince to be seated.

But Virendra stood still, staring at the ground. Tej paled. What was happening to him? His face was pale, his eyes stony. He did not seem to be aware of anything. It was as if he had died along with Chandrakanta. Tej caught hold of his hand and tried to make him sit down, but the prince's knees remained stiff. Then suddenly he toppled over, knocking his head on the ground. Blood flowed from the wound, but his eyes remained fixed and his breath began to falter.

Tej began to weep bitterly. Would the prince survive this blow? Devi broke down too.

'Oh, my friend, are you really leaving us?' Tej wailed. 'What evil moment was that when your love for Chandrakanta took birth? It had to end like this. Ah . . . your life was meant to be only this long!'

Suddenly a voice was heard, saying, 'No, the prince's life is not so short. It's extremely long, in fact. Not a single soul exists who is capable of killing him. And his love for Princess Chandrakanta—it sprang up at a very auspicious moment. She is very much alive. He will marry her and attain the throne of Chunar. He'll also conquer many other lands and two brilliant sons will be born to them. Why do you weep?'

Tej and Devi stopped wailing and looked around. Who is this, Tej thought, who sounds as if he can bring the dead back to life? But the prince seemed to be breathing his last. Both the aiyaars began to search for the source of those magical words.

'I am here!' It was the same voice.

Tej raised his head and found Jagannath the astrologer climbing down from a tree.

'Don't look so puzzled,' he said. 'I'm the one who spoke. You might wonder why I'm saying all these comforting things, being on Maharaja Shivdutt's side. You'll soon find out. But first let's take a look at the prince.'

Even as Tej and Devi watched, Jagannath plucked a herb

from the undergrowth nearby. It had triangular leaves and blue flowers growing on a coarse white stem. He rubbed it between his hands and squeezed two drops of the juice into Virendra's eyes and ears. He tore a strip from his shoulder cloth and tied what remained of the plant to the soles of the prince's feet. Then he waited for it to take effect.

Hardly a moment had passed when the prince's eyelids dropped over his staring eyes. Slowly, his hands and feet began to move. Then he sneezed a few times and sat up.

'Well? What happened to me?' he asked, frowning at the three men who sat there gazing at him anxiously.

Tej told him everything. The prince bowed to the astrologer and said, 'Maharaj, why have you been so good to me? It's making me suspicious.'

'It is all God's will,' Jagannath replied, folding his hands. 'I would like to join your group. Maharaja Shivdutt is not the kind of man for whom I would risk my life. He is without principles and cannot discriminate between good and bad. He values a man only for what he has accomplished, by whatever means possible. Any decent human being would shun him. If I have to serve anyone, it can only be you. Luckily, I found an opportunity today, when you were in great danger, all through his evil manipulations.'

The last words startled them all. They moved closer to Jagannath and Tej said, 'Tell us clearly. Why did Shivdutt resort to this trick?'

'The king always consults me before embarking on any great enterprise,' Jagannath replied. 'However, he ultimately does what he wishes. I told him this was not a good plan. And see what happened? Ghasita and Bhagwandutt lost their lives. I'll tell you everything—only if you take me on your side.'

The prince exchanged glances with Tej. 'Jagannathji, I'll be too happy to agree,' Tej replied. 'But you'll have to swear an oath of fealty.'

The astrologer took his sacred thread in his hand and swore he would be true to them. Tej rose and embraced him as a sign that he was part of their band now. Virendra took off a valuable necklace and put it around Jagannath's neck.

'Now let me tell you the real reason why the prince was imprisoned in the palace,' the astrologer began. 'That night, when you left your camp to search for the princess, Badrinath saw you. Immediately, he set off for the cave where she was imprisoned, to shift her to another place. But the princess was gone. Frustrated, he returned to the forest with Nazim, who threw stones to divert Devi. Then Badrinath disguised himself as Tej and captured the prince. They decided to fool you into believing that Chandrakanta no longer cared for you so you would abandon your search and end your quarrel with Shivdutt. Therefore the two youngest aiyaars, Bhagwandutt and Ghasita, were made up to look like the two girls. The rest you know.'

'What shameless deceit!' the prince exclaimed. 'Ah, at least Chandrakanta is alive. Wherever she might be, we can hope to find her.'

After some discussion, they decided to confine Shivdutt

in Tej's secret prison. Virendra was advised to return to Vijaygarh to keep an eye on things there, and Devi to accompany him. Tej and the astrologer went off to search for Chandrakanta.

The House of Wonders

The afternoon sun shone bright. Two lovely girls were seated on a rock near a stream. Their saris were torn and soiled, their faces covered with dust, their hair dishevelled and their feet begrimed. They looked confused and troubled, surrounded as they were by the dense forest, which resounded with the calls of wild animals. Even the rustling of the leaves in the wind sounded menacing in that lonely spot and made them shiver with fear.

A leopard appeared on the opposite bank, to drink from the stream. 'Dear friend,' said the delicate-looking girl to her friend, 'I hope it doesn't cross over!'

'Don't worry,' said the other. 'If it does, I'll fell it with my arrows.'

'But Chapla,' the first continued, 'where are we? How can we locate the road to Vijaygarh?'

'I'm afraid I have no idea,' Chapla said. 'When we escaped, my only concern was to get away from that place as fast as possible. And since I have mostly stayed in the palace with you, hardly ever left Vijaygarh, I don't know these forests at all. I'm familiar with the road from Chunar, but it would not be safe. The enemy's on the prowl there. But . . . would you like something to eat?'

'We can pluck some berries,' Chandrakanta said. 'We don't have much choice.'

The girls wandered through the forest looking for wild fruit. Afternoon had shaded into evening when they came across a ruined mansion. Chapla suggested that the princess rest at the door while she gathered more berries. 'If by chance a traveller or herdsman passes this way we can ask for the way to Vijaygarh.'

For a while Chandrakanta sat at the door. But she began to feel nervous all alone. So she decided to distract herself by exploring the ruins.

There was something very impressive about the house, dilapidated though it was. The doorframe at the entrance was still intact, though the doors had disappeared. When she entered, the princess noticed that it was a large square structure. A little further in, she found a courtyard. The roof had fallen in, leaving only the pillars standing. Stepping carefully over the piles of stones and bricks that lay everywhere, she came to a wide, open space. It must have been a garden, she thought, noticing some remnants of marble-edged flowerbeds. Nearby were little channels for water, and broken fountains covered with a thick sheet of mud. Chandrakanta's eyes grew wide when she discovered a huge stone crane right in the middle of the ruins. She went nearer, exclaiming at the exquisite workmanship.

It was made of white marble and set on a pedestal of black stone as high as her waist. The legs were not visible and it seemed to be crouching on its stomach, which was about fifteen hands in circumference. The long beak and feathers were so delicately carved that she wanted to examine them more minutely. But the moment she drew closer, it suddenly opened its mouth. Alarmed, Chandrakanta stepped aside. The bird then spread its wings.

Chandrakanta did not believe in ghosts and magic because Chapla had convinced her that all these things were deliberately created illusions. So this action did not terrify her, as it might have another girl. When the crane spread its wings, she moved behind it. Accidentally, she stepped on a stone slab. Immediately, the bird's head swung around. Its beak opened and it swallowed Chandrakanta!

Then it went back to its original position.

Chapla returned with a bag full of fruit and was puzzled to find the princess gone. She looked around, then entered the ruins to search for her. But while the princess had walked through impetuously, Chapla took her time and examined everything. She observed two courtyards side by side, the piles of stones, the broken roof, but noticed that the statues and the pictures on the walls still looked new.

Further ahead she saw more statues, badly damaged, with heads and other parts missing. Their appearance was fearsome. Then she arrived at the open space where the stone crane stood. As she hurried up to it, curious, it opened its beak. Astonished, Chapla stepped back and its mouth closed. This made her stop and think. It seemed a remarkable device. What was its secret? But she had to find the princess first. It was possible she had got trapped in some similar contraption.

So she left that spot and began to look around. There were several courtyards with rooms around them, some ruined, some intact. She entered one about a hundred yards long, with heaps of mud and bones in the middle and cobwebs all around. Saplings of trees like the peepul had taken root there. She turned into a small room and discovered that there was a well inside.

The place appeared cleaner than the rest of the area and she could hear strange sounds from the well. Since it was hard to see anything clearly, Chapla took some pieces of camphor out of her bag, lit them and dropped them inside. Camphor has this quality—it continues to burn when dropped in a well or pit. Now that it was brighter, she saw that there was no water in the well. A clean white sheet was spread at the bottom and an old man sat on it. His long beard was visible, but since his head was bent she could not see his face. A low stool lay before him and some colourful flowers were strewn on it. For a moment Chapla experienced a chill of fear. Then she collected herself and tried to make sense out of all this, but it seemed impossible. In the meantime the bits of camphor went out and it was dark again.

Defeated, Chapla made her way to another courtyard. It was filthier than the first and the skeleton of an animal lay among the heaps of bones. She went past it to explore a marble platform that stood in the middle of the courtyard. It had nine beautifully fashioned steps leading up and a man lay on a chair, holding a book. But it was too high to make out anything. Chapla wondered if she should climb the stairs to take a better look. Gingerly, she put one foot on the first step. It sprang open with a loud noise. She was thrown off and fell to the ground. The step closed up again, much like the lid of a box.

This ruined house was full of extraordinary surprises! Surely it was the work of a great aiyaar. One would have to be very careful going around. Was her dear Chandrakanta trapped somewhere inside? But Chapla was eager to discover what kind of mechanism worked the steps. She took a heavy stone about ten seers in weight and placed it on the first step. Again it sprang open and the stone was flung off. She tried placing stones on each of the steps, with the same result.

Finally, she made a pile of stones and bricks and climbed it. The stone figure on the platform was of a young man, maybe thirty years old. Chapla threw a pebble at its face. To her surprise it lifted a hand and removed it. Similarly, when she put one on its foot, it shook it off. Unnerved, she hurriedly moved on to the next courtyard.

There she came upon a flight of stairs that seemed to be leading into a cellar. She wanted to explore the place. But what if the door on top of the stairs shut itself and locked her inside? Suppose she threw a clod on the steps to see if that might happen? On the other hand, if the door closed she would not be able to go in. There was no question of wrenching it out. The door was made of heavy iron.

Chapla untied the rope at her waist, doubled it twice over, then tied one end to the door and the other to a pillar in the courtyard. Then she threw a large stone inside. The moment she did this, there was a whooshing sound and one of the doors shut. The other moved too but was held back by the rope. Now that she knew the door was secure, Chapla entered boldly.

Champa Gets into Trouble

When many days had passed and there was no news of Chandrakanta, the loyal Champa took permission from the queen to go and search for her. She wandered through dense forests, went up and down hills and valleys, but did not discover anything. Exhausted, disheartened, she sat down under a tree, wondering what to do next. Suddenly she noticed four uniformed men approaching, carrying swords and shields.

The moment they set eyes on Champa, they stopped. After a whispered exchange, they too sat down, placing themselves around her. Champa rose and began to walk away. But they jumped to their feet and blocked her way. One even tried to grab her hand. Immediately, Champa drew her dagger and fought back, wounding a couple of them. Then she took to her heels. Unluckily, she tripped on a stone and the men caught up with her.

Before the men could speak, a large caravan came into view. An opulently dressed old man who looked around eighty led it, riding a thoroughbred horse. A young boy clad like a prince followed him, along with about two hundred merchants. Many palanquins accompanied them too, guarded by soldiers. Camels carrying goods, along with men on foot, brought up the rear.

'This woman has wounded two of us,' Champa's captors called out. Right away several men surrounded her, snatched her dagger and handcuffed her.

'We can camp here in the forest,' said the old man, dismounting. 'It's quite deserted.'

Tents were set up and a rough fence erected. To Champa's astonishment, women emerged from the palanquins, and were herded into the enclosure. When it grew dark, some maids appeared and lit lamps.

'Would you like to cook your own food, or shall we get something for you?' they asked.

Most of the women asked them to fetch food. But Champa and another woman refused to eat anything. This woman was a delicate-looking beauty, her eyes streaming constantly with tears. The night progressed and the camp sank into a silence punctuated only by the steady thud of footsteps. Champa gathered that it was the guards on their rounds.

'Who are you? How did you fall into these men's clutches?' Champa asked softly.

'I'm Kalavati,' said the woman, 'Maharaja Shivdutt of Chunar's queen. He was away fighting a battle and I was asleep in the palace. Then I found myself a prisoner. I don't know how.'

'You're the queen of Chunar? Strange are the ways of fortune! Perhaps you know Princess Chandrakanta. I'm one of her companions. I was searching for her when these people captured me.'

Intrigued by this coincidence, the two talked through the night. At daybreak the same maids appeared, armed with swords. They took the women out to perform their toilets. But Champa and the queen did not stir and no one bothered them.

The morning was well advanced when the leader appeared with an old woman.

'These are all we have,' the man said. 'With your kind assistance the number will increase.'

'Wait and see,' the old woman leered meaningfully. 'But tell me what you'll pay for which kind of woman.'

The leader pointed to some and said, 'For this kind you'll get ten rupees.' Then he gestured towards Champa, 'For her kind, fifty.' Then he indicated the queen, 'If you come up with such a beauty you'll get a full hundred rupees.'

'From where did you get them?' asked the old woman.

'Oh, various places. But come, let's talk in my tent. My old legs are weary.'

The moment they left, the women began to curse the old hag wholeheartedly. The queen started to weep again. But

Champa, who had observed the old woman closely, remained lost in thought.

She tried to cheer the queen up. 'Don't worry, God willing, we'll soon be set free. Oh . . . if only I could cut away these fetters. I'd show these fellows a trick or two.'

The old woman reappeared with a lovely young maiden in the evening, and was rewarded with fifty rupees. 'Tomorrow I'll bring another,' she said.

Oddly, the new woman seemed quite cheerful. She gobbled down a hearty dinner and teased the other women for being so glum. Champa became convinced that she was not a regular captive like them.

The next morning, she stayed back in the camp again with the queen. 'Have you eaten at all since they captured you?' she asked her.

'I nibble a bite every second or third day, just to keep myself alive,' Kalavati sighed.

A little while later, they were forced to go out and sit under the trees. Late in the afternoon, the old woman appeared with a young woman even lovelier than the first. Champa examined her closely, then said, looking away, 'Stand I under.'

The other frowned, rubbed one of her toes and said, 'Life silence means.'

After dinner was over and the night well advanced, all the women fell asleep except Champa, the queen and the new arrivals. 'Cut or cat is out,' Champa said meaningfully.

'Happen what?' one said.

'Queen care,' Champa replied.

The first woman took out a sharp instrument from her bag and slowly sawed Champa's fetters away. Champa rubbed her feet, smiling smugly. But the next moment fierce shouts were heard. Someone had surrounded the enclosure! Panic-stricken, the women began to mill about.

'Champa!' the queen called out, terrified. 'Where are you?'

'She's gone,' one of the women said softly. 'Don't worry, your majesty. We've come to rescue you. It's our people attacking. Please wait here while we fetch a palanquin.'

They slipped out and after a while, two masked men arrived with a palanquin. The queen hurriedly stepped into it and was carried away.

The night passed and the sky began to lighten. The rest of the women were sitting there, frozen with fear, when Pannalal, Chunnilal and Ramnarayan appeared with a fine-looking palanquin curtained with brocade. They began to search among them.

'Don't be afraid,' Pannalal said. 'You're free now. But we're looking for two women who don't seem to be here.'

'If you're looking for the four who were together,' a woman said, 'one disappeared when the confusion began. The other two told the fourth that they were bringing a palanquin for her. When it arrived, she too left.'

The three men gazed at each other, stunned. 'Who could have taken her away?' Ramnarayan said. 'Let's see if any of the slave traders' palanquins are missing. And let these women out too.'

The old man, his son and all the other traders were safely in chains. But when Ramnarayan counted the palanquins, he found one missing.

'Champa could not have managed this without help,' he said, shaking his head. 'And the old man is our prisoner, so he can't be involved. What a loss! Four days' hard work has come to nought.'

Chunnilal then fetched the chief minister of Chunar, who was leading the army. 'Please take the captives back to the city,' Pannalal said. 'We'll search for the queen.'

'That Champa outwitted us,' Chunnilal said. 'I thought we'd get hold of her too.'

'Well, I wonder what laurels Ahmed, Nazim and Badrinath are going to win,' Ramnarayan said. 'They were supposed to find his majesty.'

'We certainly haven't won any,' said Pannalal.

'The person who carried the queen away is far ahead of us,' Ramnarayan said despondently. 'We might as well give up.'

After some more talk, the three set off in different directions.

*

Tej Singh and Jagannath were sitting by a wide stream in the forest, near the palanquin bearing Queen Kalavati. Champa stood close by.

'I do not wish to return to Chunar,' said the queen. 'I'd rather stay with my husband, wherever he may be.'

'Your majesty, I'm the only one who can take you there,' Tej said. 'But think again. The king is likely to be in prison for a long time.'

Kalavati simply said, 'I'll be very grateful if you reunite us.'

'But you can't go there in this palanquin,' Tej said. 'I'll have to make you unconscious.'

The queen agreed readily. When she lay there senseless, the astrologer said, 'You take her to the cave, I'll stay here and Champa can return to Vijaygarh.'

'I'll stay here and search for the princess and Chapla,' said Champa. 'I may have got caught by the traffickers, but I escaped without your help.'

'We're not claiming that,' Tej said. 'We came to look for Chandrakanta. By chance we saw the queen, and the Chunar aiyaars trying to free her. We thought we'd make use of the opportunity. But how long will you keep searching? Suppose we find her and you continue, unaware?'

'Don't worry about that!' Champa's mouth set firmly.

Tej gave up and left with the queen. Champa went her way, and the astrologer remained in the forest.

After a while, he thought of using his tools of divination to discover the two girls' whereabouts. He pulled out his wooden tablet and began to make calculations. Suddenly, his face lit up. He quickly gathered up his things and ran after Tej.

Tej Singh was walking at full speed. He had already covered ten miles when he heard someone call, 'Stop! Stop!'

Seeing Jagannath, he became apprehensive. Then he noticed the smile on his face.

'I'm coming with you to the cavern,' Jagannath said.

'Why?'

'I'll tell you when we get there.'

'I'll have to blindfold you. I cannot let out the secret of the lock.'

'I refuse,' said the astrologer. 'And you'll have to take me.'

'But why?'

'Because I've found the answer. Princess Chandrakanta's there.'

'Tell the truth.'

'If it's a lie, you can kill me.'

'Certainly, and take on the sin of killing a brahmin,' Tej said. 'Well, come along. I guess I have to obey you.'

The next evening, they reached the secret prison. Tej pulled out the lion's tongue and opened the first lock. Then he kicked a marble slab embedded on the right side of the door. The stone sank to the ground with a loud groan and a small platform appeared. A snake sat coiled on it. Tej twisted its neck several times, like you rotate a screw. The door swung open and he entered with the queen. Jagannath followed. Then Tej closed the door and put his hand in a small hole in the wall. He did something the astrologer could not see.

'What's in there?' he asked.

'A small screw. When you turn it, the stone I kicked slips

back into its place. But you cannot open the door with it. You have to follow the same method I used outside,' Tej said.

When they reached the meadow, Tej let the queen out from the bundle and asked her to follow them.

But he was eager to find the princess. 'So . . . where is Chandrakanta?' he asked Jagannath.

'I don't know . . . exactly. Locate the king and we'll discover Chandrakanta too.'

They reached the stream and came upon Shivdutt. He was standing there, gazing up at something. The queen was so overjoyed that she plunged into the stream without a second thought. Luckily it was quite shallow. She crossed it and ran to the king, who embraced her. By that time the other two had also reached too.

'What are you doing here?' Shivdutt asked Jagannath. 'Has Tej Singh snared you?'

'No, I've joined him,' the astrologer said. 'I'm on Virendra's side now.'

The king's eyes flashed with anger but Jagannath said, 'What's the use of getting angry? Have you forgotten the harsh words you flung at me? I prefer to stay with someone who respects me.'

Shivdutt's face fell.

Just then they heard a faint voice call, 'Tej Singh!'

Tej looked up and saw Chandrakanta standing outside a small cave on top of the hill. Her plight brought tears to his eyes. Her face looked wan, her clothes were torn and dirty. He ran and tried to climb up and get to her. However, the slope was too steep. He took out his rope and flung it up, but it was too short. Jagannath took out his rope, they tied the two together, but they only reached halfway.

Frustrated, Tej flung them down and asked, 'How did you get there?'

The words, 'Fate . . . came . . . way . . . came out,' reached his ears. He could see the princess's lips moving, but could not hear anything else.

'I'll find a way,' Tej shouted back.

Chandrakanta looked around, plucked a broad leaf from a tree and scratched something on it with a sharp stone. Then tearing a strip from her sari, she tied it to another stone and threw it down. Tej retrieved it from the stream where it landed, and read it eagerly.

'Bring the prince here first,' it said.

'I'm going to fetch the prince,' Tej said, showing the leaf to Jagannath. 'Please stay here and see if you can find a way to get her out.'

He hurried from the grotto.

Virendra Enters the Fray

Chandrakanta's disappearance had plunged not only her parents and the palace retainers into gloom, but the whole city of Vijaygarh mourned with them.

When Virendra returned with Devi Singh, everyone hoped that Chandrakanta would follow soon. But after hearing about their adventures, Jai Singh became even more worried. The news that Shivdutt had been captured did cheer him up. However, he lost all hope of his daughter's return now. Hardayal tried to convince him that Tej would surely rescue her, even if it were from hell, but his words were to no avail.

After visiting his parents once, Virendra stayed on in Vijaygarh, restless and miserable. One night, as he was tossing and turning in his bed, he heard someone say, 'the prince'. Curious to know who was discussing him, he crept to the door.

It was the guards. 'Whether you agree or not, at first I believed that Prince Virendra truly loved the princess,' he overheard. 'But now I'm convinced he's only interested in acquiring Vijaygarh. If he really cared for her, wouldn't he be out searching?'

Just then, a sound disturbed them and they moved away to investigate. The prince stood there for a long time, but heard no more.

The words pierced his heart. If these common soldiers believed he was an opportunist, the king and the queen must surely be thinking the same. I can't stay here any longer, he thought. I must do something.

The next morning, after getting dressed and having his breakfast, he sent for his horse and left the fort. Several men hurried up asking to accompany him, but he shook his head firmly. Devi, however, could not be brushed off so easily. Virendra spurred his horse on, but being an aiyaar, Devi kept pace. Besides, it was not easy for the horse to move fast on the rocky terrain.

Eventually, the prince took pity and reined in his steed. He waited there laughing, as Devi scrambled up.

'Just tell me one thing,' Devi said panting, 'are you out of your mind?'

The prince jumped off. 'Let the horse graze,' he said, 'and listen to what I have to say.'

The two sat down and Virendra told him what he had overheard. 'I will not return to either Vijaygarh or Naugarh till I find Chandrakanta,' he said.

'Do you think you'll do a better job than us?' Devi frowned. 'Tej and the astrologer are already looking for her. You should go back to Naugarh. It's quite close by.'

'No it isn't,' said the prince.

'You were so lost in thought that you hardly watched where you were going. See, there's the large peepul tree that lies close to the cavern in which Shivdutt is locked up. And, oh, look there's Tej. I'm sure he has some news.'

Tej was still quite far away, but the prince could not wait. He ran to meet him.

'Do you have any news?' Virendra asked impatiently.

'Yes, come with me.'

Overjoyed, the prince hugged Tej tightly. 'Where is she?'

'At a spot . . . near the cave,' Tej said.

'Let's go then!' Virendra leapt on to his horse.

*

'There she is,' Tej pointed out, when they were inside the grotto.

The prince gazed up at her. His face bloomed with happiness. But when Chandrakanta gazed back, holding out her arms helplessly, anxiety replaced his joy.

Like Tej, he tried to dash up the hill. But after several unsuccessful forays, he realized it was impossible.

'If there had been a way, wouldn't I have got her down?'

Tej sighed. He turned to the astrologer. 'Have you discovered any solution?'

'Not yet,' Jagannath said. 'My divination reveals that she can return only by the route she reached there. That's not so simple either. Someone has created a kind of maze and she's caught in it. It has to be penetrated in a particular manner.'

'A maze?' Tej's eyes gleamed at the challenge. 'Please don't get anxious!' he called out to the princess. 'Just tell us how you got there.'

Chapla's Incredible Journey

Chapla climbed into the cellar. She found a large chamber, which had a doorframe but no doors. She entered carefully but the moment she stepped in, a large iron door came down with a bang.

'What is this, a mousetrap?' she thought, looking back in dismay.

It had turned pitch dark and she had to grope her way. Suddenly, her foot sank into a hole. A loud sound startled her. Then she saw that another door had opened, letting in some moonlight. She stepped out into a somewhat unkempt garden. Noticing a pavilion in the distance, she headed towards it.

The pavilion was constructed of black stone. The roof,

floor and pillars were all ink black. A marble throne lay right in the centre, on which a square red stone was placed. When Chapla examined it, she found the following words engraved on it:

This is tilism, a magical maze. Those trapped here cannot escape on their own. Only he who knows how to solve its mystery can set them free and obtain the treasure. But only the strongest will succeed.

Chapla now knew that she could never retrace her steps. Even her attempt to hold the first door open with the rope had proved futile. Perhaps the door through which she had entered the garden might still be open.

But no trace of the door or doorway remained. Puzzled, she returned to the pavilion. On an impulse, she thought of picking up the red stone. If she managed to get out, it would be something worth showing.

She bent to pick it up. But as soon as she touched it, a current shook her frame, her head whirled and she fell to the ground unconscious.

*

When Chapla returned to her senses, she was astonished to see that the sun was setting. Had she been asleep the whole day? She washed her face in one of the water channels and felt refreshed. Grapes clustered profusely on the vines in the garden, but she was too troubled to consider eating them. Then darkness fell and she noticed a strange phenomenon.

The pavilion began to glow with an eerie light. As the night progressed, it shone brighter. Its radiance completely illuminated that portion of the garden.

Baffled, Chapla stroked the floor, walls and pillars, trying to discover the source of this light. Astonishment and alarm so affected her that she could not sleep a wink all night. Again and again she would examine the walls or look intently at the stone that had struck her unconscious.

When morning came, she decided to explore the garden further. The channel passed beneath one of the surrounding walls. The wall was not very thick and the opening of the channel was deep and broad enough for her to enter and swim through. After some thought, she plunged into it fully clothed, and came out on the other side of the wall. Here, the channel grew wider and she discovered that it flowed on through high mountains that stretched into the distance.

Chapla stepped out and dried her clothes. Her bag of tricks had not got wet, being made of waterproof fabric. She checked her equipment and when she was satisfied, set off, walking along the banks of the channel. The hills were too high to climb. She must have walked for about six miles when she came to a dead end. A hill rose before her and a waterfall spilling down it flowed into the channel. Below was a narrow courtyard, about a yard wide and ten yards long. It seemed to have been cut out of the hill. A huge stone python was positioned in the middle. Its mouth, large enough to swallow a man, gaped open. A broad, smooth marble slab lay before it.

Intrigued, Chapla went closer, then shrieked. The moment she stepped on the slab, she was jerked up. And an irresistible force dragged her towards the python's mouth! Chapla jammed her foot down hard, but to no effect. She was pulled into the python's mouth and carried into its stomach. After that, she did not know what happened.

When she came to, she found herself in a tiny room. Stairs led out of it, but for a while she was too stunned to act. Then she collected herself and climbed them. They led out into the open. Tall hills surrounded her and she saw a small tunnel before her, through which she could glimpse some light. Exhausted, distressed at her situation, she walked through it mechanically and reached another courtyard. And cried out in surprise.

Chandrakanta was seated there! Several wide leaves were arrayed before her, and she was writing on one with a pointed stone. When Chapla went closer, she noticed that they were at the edge of a steep cliff.

And the prince, Tej and Jagannath the astrologer stood below gazing up at them!

Hearing her footsteps, Chandrakanta rose and embraced her. 'At last, you've come! See, they are all there but we cannot get to them,' she sighed. 'I can hear them but they can't hear me. Tej is asking me which way I entered, so I'm writing it down.'

Chapla looked around again and realized that it really was impossible to go down. 'I can shout and tell them,' she said. 'My voice will carry. But tell me, did the crane swallow you or did you get here some other way?'

'It was the crane. You must have seen it in the ruins. Did it swallow you too?'

'No. But first we must tell them how to reach the ruins so they can set us free. I fear we'll be stuck here for a long time.'

Chapla beckoned to Tej. 'There are some old ruins, about fourteen miles south of the cave in which Shivdutt imprisoned us,' she yelled out. 'A huge stone crane, an extraordinary marvel, stands inside them. It swallowed the princess and she wandered here. If you can solve that puzzle we'll be saved. I entered with great caution but got trapped all the same. I don't know on which side of Chunar the cave lies, where the evil Shivdutt held us captive.' Chapla's voice was hoarse by the time she finished.

The last words enraged the prince. He drew his sword and turned on Shivdutt.

The queen flung herself at his feet. 'Spare him, I beg you!' she cried. 'Kill me instead!'

Tej pulled him away. 'Don't dissipate your energy!' he said. 'We have to rescue Chandrakanta.'

They decided to inform Jai Singh about his daughter's whereabouts and try to find the right way to enter the mysterious ruins.

'Take good care of the princess,' Tej called to Chapla. 'It may take some time to penetrate this labyrinth.'

'Don't worry,' Chapla replied. 'There are plenty of berries and wild fruit here and streams to drink from. You need to be very cautious. But this much I have gathered—only the prince can unravel the mystery of this tilism. You must take good care of him.'

Into the Maze

When Virendra left without a word, Maharaja Jai Singh was beside himself with anxiety. He immediately sent spies to search, but none of them could trace the prince.

Consequently, he was overwhelmed with relief when Virendra returned on his own along with Tej Singh. The quick-witted Tej explained that the prince had had to leave early for pressing reasons and did not wish to disturb anyone. Then he informed Jai Singh about all that had occurred.

The king was wonderstruck. 'You've performed extraordinary deeds, no doubt,' he said. 'But these mysterious ruins lie in another's territory. Shivdutt may be your prisoner, but you must arm yourself well and ... be extremely careful.'

Since Jai Singh was curious to see the ruins too, they decided to leave with a properly equipped force. Devi, who had been sent to Naugarh, came back, and they set off for Chunar the next day.

On the fifth day they arrived at the Chunar border. Shivdutt being their prisoner, this created much anxiety. The prime minister, who was officiating in the king's absence, hurried to them, bearing gifts. They assured him that they had no designs on Chunar, but other plans.

Strangely, no one in Chunar knew about these extraordinary ruins. The news that Prince Virendra had arrived to unravel a tilism spread rapidly. Spies were pressed into service along with the aiyaars, and the ruins were soon located. The Vijaygarh forces set up camp near them.

With some trepidation and much excitement, Jai Singh, Virendra, Tej, Devi and the astrologer entered the mysterious house. They gazed up at the crane that had swallowed the princess. Tej Singh held the others back and inched forward cautiously, the way Chapla had.

To their astonishment, the crane opened its beak. They watched as it spread its wings and turned around.

'What extraordinary brain created this wonder!' the king said, wide-eyed.

Following Chapla's steps, the group arrived at the entrance of the cellar. Tej noticed the door Chapla had secured with her rope. They examined the well and came to the platform where the sleeping man reclined with his book. Like Chapla, Tej tried to climb the steps and was flung back.

Virendra laughed at the sight, but Devi became furious. He leapt up and hit the stone man on its head.

Immediately the figure sat up and opened its mouth. A kind of a vapour emerged from it and the ground began to shudder.

'Hurry, it's not safe to remain here!' Jagannath shouted. They all ran for their lives.

The ruins continued to shake for a good two hours even after they got out.

'Can't you divine how this mystery might be solved?' Tej asked the astrologer. 'And who will solve it?'

'I'll do it tonight,' Jagannath said. 'But the task might stretch over several days, so it's better that his majesty leaves now.'

Jai Singh departed, somewhat unwillingly, with half the troops. Jagannath stayed up all night, making calculations and trying to figure out his findings. The others kept him company. Finally the astrologer said, 'The key to penetrating this maze successfully is engraved on a stone that lies somewhere within the ruins. Once we locate it, we can get on with the job.'

After they had bathed, performed their puja and eaten, they made for the ruins. They reached the platform where the stone man lay and found him back in the reclining position again.

'This pile of stones must have been collected by Chapla,' Jagannath said. 'Tej, why don't you climb up and examine the book carefully? See what's written in it.'

Tej did so. He read out aloud:

'8 sides—5—numbers

6 hands—3—fingers

Accumulated fund—0—add,

Correct measure breaks!

But what could all this mean?'

'Take it down on a piece of paper. We'll work it out,' Jagannath replied.

Tej took out paper, pen and ink from his bag and copied the inscription.

'Now let's see if there is an eight-sided pillar or platform anywhere,' the astrologer said, after going over it again.

They searched everywhere unsuccessfully, and then stopped at the courtyard where the cellar lay. As they were gazing at the rope Chapla had fastened to the door to keep it open, they noticed that the pillar on which the other end was tied had eight sides. This pillar was not attached to a roof. Jagannath said, 'Let us measure its height.'

They all tried. When Tej measured it, it came to six hands and seven finger lengths, Devi, six hands and five fingers, Jagannath, six hands and ten fingers, but when the prince measured it, it was exactly six hands and three fingers.

Jagannath beamed. 'We've found it! The pillar has eight sides and see, there's a five inscribed here. The "accumulated fund"—the stone on which the key to solving the mystery is engraved—is buried beneath it. We also know now that only the prince can accomplish this task, since his measurement was the correct one. Now Tej, will you untie the rope, so we can proceed?'

Tej did so. Virendra picked up a large, hard chunk of lime plaster. He threw it at the pillar with such force that it shook. Two or three such blows weakened it. Then the prince put his arms around it, heaved with all his strength and uprooted it. The pillar fell over, revealing an iron chest. After much effort, Virendra managed to break the lock. Another chest lay inside it—and another lock to be broken. In this manner, the prince encountered seven chests altogether.

The seventh contained a stone on which was written:

If your name is Virendra Singh, proceed with caution. Do not be too hasty in solving this mystery.

The stone that lies in front of the crane is not really made of marble but a kind of plaster. Pull it out and grind it to a fine paste with vinegar. Apply the paste on the crane. It will dissolve, leaving a mechanism of wires and wheels. Break everything and you will find a chamber below it. It leads to the bottom of the well where you will see an old man with a book in his hand. You have to remove this book in a particular way. First, grasp his right arm and he will open his mouth. Fill his mouth with camphor. The figure will disintegrate and you can take the book. The pages are made of birch bark. Follow the instructions given in the book.

Vikram

The prince read this aloud. Dumbfounded, they could not help praising the ingenuity of the person who created this house of wonders. But it was growing dark and they decided it would be better to go back to the camp and return the next day.

News had spread through the whole Chunar region that there was a tilism, a mysterious maze in a ruin in which Princess Chandrakanta and Chapla were trapped. And that Prince Virendra was trying to save them.

What is a tilism? How does a person get caught in it? Why did the prince want to unravel the mystery? These were the questions that attracted people from far and near. They hung around the camp watching, but did not dare to step into the ruins.

Virendra's men also reported that a group of masked horsemen had been seen roaming the place.

In the meantime, the Chunar aiyaars, Badrinath, Ahmed and Nazim, went to Tej's secret prison and tried to free Shivdutt. But Badrinath was unable to open the double lock. Frustrated, they decided to prevent the prince from conquering the maze.

The following morning, the prince and his group entered the ruins carrying some vinegar. They uprooted the white stone in front of the crane, ground it with vinegar and applied the paste to the crane. It began to disintegrate, along with its pedestal, giving out a strange odour. After two hours, they found a chamber beneath it. They cut away all the wires and metal parts that hung there and descended to find the old man in the well. The moment the prince grasped the figure's right arm, it opened its mouth. Tej, who had already lit a large torch, held out the camphor and Virendra stuffed it into its mouth. It took an hour for the old man to dissolve away. The book fell on the ground and Virendra picked it up. There was something written on its cover, which like the pages was of birch bark.

The prince read it out:

Pick up these flowers. They will be of great help to your aiyaars. Their qualities are described in the book. Take it back to your camp and read it. Do not do anything else today.

Tej quickly picked up the six brightly coloured stone flowers, the same that Chapla had marvelled at, and they made their way back to the camp.

At first they decided to read the book at night, when no one was around. But Tej was desperate to learn the qualities of the flowers.

'We'll read that portion only after the mystery has been solved.' Virendra laughed teasingly.

However, Tej pleaded so much that he gave in. They asked all the attendants to depart and the prince began to read out:

The Amazing Qualities of the Stone Flowers
1. *Rose—if ground into a paste with water and drunk, it will act as a guard against any kind of knock-out drug.*
2. *Motia—if ground and added to a well, anyone who drinks*

water from it will fall unconscious for twelve hours. Its effect will manifest itself after half an hour.

The aiyaars jumped with excitement. The prince closed the book and said, 'I won't read any more.'

'Please!' Tej folded his hands. 'You are the one who'll benefit.'

Virendra went on teasing Tej for a while, then he continued:

3. *Oruhar—if you make a paste and drink it, you will not feel hungry for four days.*
4. *Oleander—if you wash your feet with a paste made from this flower, the exhaustion of a long journey will immediately vanish.*
5. *Chrysanthemum—a paste made from this flower and applied to the eyes will enable you to see in the dark.*
6. *Kewra—if ground into a paste with oil, it will protect you against cold, with water, heat and sunlight will not affect you, and with catechu water, anyone who drinks it will lose all his energy for one week.*

Tej rubbed his hands in glee and promptly put all the flowers into his bag. Jagannath and Devi kept asking him to share them, but he would not let them take even a look.

Tej was so elated at acquiring these flowers that it seemed he had never been happier in his life. He was already a great aiyaar and these would add considerably to his powers. He felt that no one could equal him now. If he had any regrets, it was that he had not been able to find a powder or ointment that would make him invisible. But on the other hand, he thought, it would not bring him much glory if he had, because his skill would never be put to test.

They spent the night poring over the book, discussing it and the qualities of the extraordinary flowers.

When they got ready to leave for the ruins in the morning, the prince told Tej, 'Can you bring the book? It's lying on my bed. We'll consult it again when we're there.'

Tej took a long time to return. 'The book isn't there,' he frowned. 'I've looked under the bed, searched all over the tent—to no avail.'

The prince paled. 'How can that be?' he cried, rushing to his tent. He shook up his bedding, flung everything around, but there was no sign of the book. Overcome with despair, he slumped on to his bed. How would he enter the maze and rescue Chandrakanta now? The others sat there silent, stunned.

Finally Devi rose. 'Let's look in other parts of the camp,' he said.

'Don't lose hope,' Tej squeezed Virendra's shoulder. 'I'll catch the thief, I promise. If you give up, how will we carry on?'

The prince was just getting to his feet, when a sentry came and said, 'Your highness, someone's entered the ruins! A guard has heard sounds!'

'Hurry!' Tej cried. Devi rushed out and the others followed.

As they burst through the gate, loud shouts came to their ears. Swiftly, they made their way to the courtyard where the stone man reclined with his book and halted, surprised.

The man was sitting up, clutching Badrinath in his hands. The alarmed aiyaar was yelling as Pannalal, Ramnarayan and Chunnilal struggled to set him free.

Virendra's gloom fled as he burst into peals of laughter. The others followed.

'Wonderful!' Tej said. 'This is what you get for harassing the prince. Why are you taking such risks, Pannalal? Leave him to cool his heels while you enjoy yourself.'

'How can we abandon him?' Pannalal scowled. 'Do what you wish. We'll put up with it.'

'My respects, panditji,' Tej bowed to Badrinath. 'Why didn't you set your king free first? Maybe you want to appropriate the treasure and rule Chunar yourself.'

Devi mocked the aiyaar in the same vein and Jagannath said, 'Your stars are against you. Kindly return our book. Your luck might change then.'

Badrinath remained silent, with his eyes fixed to the ground. His companions appealed to the prince to save him. But Virendra replied, 'I cannot do anything till you return the book.'

Badrinath and Pannalal exchanged glances. 'We haven't stolen your book,' the latter said. 'Please allow us to bring him some food at least.'

'That's very well,' Devi said. 'But what if he needs to answer the call of nature?'

Pannalal could make no reply. 'Well, even if the prince does not give permission, I do,' Tej said. 'You've created a lot of problems for us. But I swear I'll wrest the book from you, without using force.'

This made Badrinath see red. 'You're ridiculing me because I'm helpless. You think you're the only aiyaar in the world? Yes, we've taken your book. But you won't be able to get it back without a fight. If you can, we'll renounce our king and serve the prince.'

Both Tej and Badrinath then swore to abandon their profession if the other succeeded. The guards were instructed to allow the Chunar aiyaars to come and go as they pleased.

Virendra's party returned to camp, Devi and the astrologer going ahead. When Virendra and Tej reached, they found him missing.

'He's gone somewhere,' Jagannath said carelessly.

'Have you discovered where the book is?' Tej asked.

'I have divined that the Chunar aiyaars don't have it any longer. But I cannot locate it. Let's see what Devi learns.'

'Let's all go and search,' Tej said.

'First tell me why you let them off,' Virendra frowned. 'You ruined everything with your bragging.'

'I'll prove what I said,' Tej said. 'Wait and see. I'll recover the book and remain in your service too.'

The Mysterious Maiden

The prince sat glumly in his tent, battling his thoughts and waiting for the aiyaars to return. But even by late afternoon there was no sign of them. Bored and restless, he finally stomped out. Fateh Singh, who was stationed nearby, hurried behind him, fully armed.

'I'm tired of sitting around,' said the prince. 'Let's take a walk.'

They sauntered into the forest, leaving the camp far behind. Suddenly, Virendra turned to Fateh Singh. 'Fateh Singh,' he said, 'I've known you since childhood and feel I can confide in you. I'm terribly distressed at Tej's rash behaviour. He let Badrinath off just when the Chunar people were in our grasp. Oh . . . I wonder if I'll ever be reunited with Chandrakanta!'

'Don't lose hope,' Fateh said gently. 'Tej knows what he's doing. Wait and see, they'll all join you soon. He's entrusted me with a task too, which seems to be going well.'

Just then, a group of women appeared, leading horses. Mystified, the two watched them, staying out of sight behind some trees. There were about twenty of them. One was particularly beautiful. Around fifteen years of age, with a finely etched face, she was dressed richly like a princess, and covered with jewels from head to toe.

Virendra's eyes remained fixed on her. 'What a graceful form,' he said. 'She looks a bit like Chandrakanta. She must be educated too; she's carrying a book in her hand. Who could this Bankanya, this forest maiden, be?'

When the group came closer, Virendra got a clearer view. The girl halted to glance at the book and tears suddenly fell from her eyes.

And then he recognized the book! 'Tilism' was inscribed on it in golden letters. How did the book fall into her hands and why was she crying?

As the prince watched, Bankanya stopped and turned around. A lively looking woman who was behind her came forward and handed her a picture. Bankanya passed the book to her. She gazed at the picture and began to weep again.

'Who *is* this woman?' the prince frowned.

'She looks like a princess,' Fateh said slowly.

'But Fateh, that's the book—the key to the maze!'

'How did it fall into her hands?' Fateh exclaimed.

'I'm as puzzled as you,' Virendra said. 'But there's

something even more amazing. That's my picture she's carrying.'

'That's unbelievable!' Fateh cried.

'I'm completely baffled,' Virendra said. 'Let's see where they're going.'

The two began to follow the women. They had barely gone a short distance when they heard a shout. It was Tej Singh. He looked so disturbed that the prince asked, 'What's wrong?'

'It's over. I have to part from you—for life.' He was unable to say any more as his eyes brimmed over.

Virendra was perplexed and troubled. Fateh Singh quickly took charge. He wiped Tej's tears with his handkerchief and asked, 'Won't you tell us why you're taking this drastic step?'

Tej gulped and looked Virendra straight in the eye. 'I couldn't find the book,' he said piteously. 'I have to abandon my profession. I promised.'

Both the prince and Fateh were opening their mouths to speak when Devi and Jagannath appeared. 'Don't panic, Tej,' the astrologer said. 'You may not have recovered the book, but they don't have it either.'

Hearing this Tej perked up immediately.

'Very nice,' said the prince severely. 'You cried and made me cry too. Didn't even give me a chance to tell you that I've just seen the book—with someone else.' He glanced in the direction where the women had been standing, but they had vanished.

'Who has the book?' Tej cried, agitated. 'Where is he?'

'How can I tell?' replied the prince. 'Let's head that way. Maybe we'll find them.'

The aiyaars followed the prince, who walked ahead swiftly. Questions whirled through their minds. Who had the book? If he had seen it, why didn't he take it back? But he was in such a state that they dared not ask. For three hours, they scoured the forest. Finally Virendra slumped under a tree, defeated.

'Why don't you tell us who you're looking for?' Tej asked.

'Let's return to the camp first,' Virendra said, rising.

When they reached he said, 'Let's check up on Badrinath.'

They had barely stepped in through the gate when they saw Badrinath, Pannalal, along with the others.

'Well, Tej Singh, you've lost your bet!' Pannalal cried.

'How can you say that? We are in possession of the book,' Tej replied. 'Now you have to serve Prince Virendra.'

'Show it to us first,' Badrinath said.

'If you don't have it, we do,' Tej answered.

'I know you don't. Someone else has it,' Badrinath said. 'So neither has lost.'

'How did you free yourself?' asked the prince.

'By God's grace,' Badrinath boasted. 'Pannalal placed a piece of wood on the stone man's head. He dropped me and grabbed it.'

The Chunar aiyaars left after a polite farewell. The others returned to their camp.

'Who had the book? If you saw it why didn't you grab it right away?' Tej asked.

'I don't know who she is,' Virendra said. 'But she is as beautiful as Chandrakanta. I was too overcome to act.'

Fateh Singh filled in what had happened.

'Who is this woman? When did she fall in love with the prince? And from where did she get his picture?' Tej frowned.

Jagannath brought out his divining tools but could only learn that she was a princess.

Preoccupied with Bankanya, the prince could not sleep that night. When Tej saw him slumped listlessly in bed the next morning, he guessed that Virendra had fallen in love with the mysterious girl. He held his tongue and told him that the aiyaars were going to search for the women. Virendra wanted to accompany them, but Tej insisted that he stay back with Fateh.

Virendra and Fateh saw the aiyaars off, then went and sat under a tree in the forest. The prince could talk of nothing but Bankanya.

After a while, a lovely young woman carrying a basket of flowers appeared.

'Oh, I'm really late!' she exclaimed as she went past. 'The princess will be furious. But it took so long to fashion ornaments from these wild flowers.'

Virendra's eyes gleamed. 'Do you think she's carrying them to Bankanya?'

'Who are you?' Fateh called out to the girl. 'For whom are you taking these ornaments?'

'Please, sir.' She put the basket down in front of them and

161

folded her hands. 'I'm a poor woman. I can't tell you anything else.'

A strong scent wafted from the flowers. Before either of them could speak, a masked horseman appeared. 'Be careful,' he said, 'or you'll fall unconscious soon.'

The woman sprang up and tried to run away. But Fateh Singh had grabbed her already.

'Who was that well-wisher?' asked the prince, gazing after the rider who left as suddenly as he'd arrived.

'Who knows?' Fateh replied. 'But he did us a good turn. Let's find out who this lady is.'

When the woman's face was washed with hot water back at the camp, she was revealed to be none other than Badrinath.

'Tej will decide his fate when he comes,' Virendra said. So Fateh held the aiyaar captive in his own tent.

Tej and the others arrived in the evening, worn out and disheartened. The mysterious women had not been traced.

'We'll try again tomorrow,' he said wearily.

'Well, *we've* captured an aiyaar,' Virendra smiled. 'Your old friend Badrinath!'

Tej perked up considerably. They decided to keep the aiyaar under close watch and take him to the cave prison the next morning.

Badrinath had just been handed over to the guards when a soldier came and said, 'A masked rider has brought a letter for the prince.'

The prince glanced at Tej, then shrugged and opened the letter. It said:

He for whom I abandoned comfort and delight
That stone-hearted one is oblivious to my plight
Forsaking my royal state,
I'll turn ascetic, smear myself with ash
Flame in the fire of separation from my love, alas!

'Hurry, call back the messenger!' the prince cried, his voice choked. But the man had vanished.

'Don't grieve,' Tej said. 'We may not have found her, but she seems just as much in love with you.'

'This letter has made matters worse. I can't control my longing,' Virendra sighed. 'I have no choice, however. I have to wait till tomorrow.'

The prince spent the night reading the poem over and over again. When he insisted on roaming the forest the next day with Fateh, Tej made a paste from the miraculous stone rose and asked them to drink it so no one could trick them.

The three aiyaars went their way and Virendra and Fateh theirs. After a while, they saw two of the mysterious masked horsemen again. One of them dismounted a short distance away and placed something on the ground.

'This book is for you, the letter too,' he said and rode off.

'The book!' Virendra cried, picking it up. 'But . . . he sounded like a woman.'

He tore open the letter. 'The one you love is trapped in the maze,' he read. 'If she is troubled, you will be unhappy. Your happiness means my happiness. For this reason I'm returning the book to you. Conquer the maze and save

Chandrakanta. But don't forget me. Leave your reply in the same spot where the book was placed.'

Virendra immediately wrote:

Ever since I saw you with this book in your hand, I've been longing to meet you. I will consider myself most fortunate the day I set eyes on both my loves. But you seem to detest the sight of my face.

Yours ever,
Virendra.

He set the letter down in the same spot and waited, but the two riders did not approach. Only when the prince moved away did one pick up the letter. Then they rode off and were lost to sight.

Mystified, Virendra and Fateh returned to the camp.

When night fell, Tej dragged himself in dispiritedly. 'No luck,' he said. 'We glimpsed some masked horsemen near the camp, but they evaded us cleverly. Tomorrow we'll definitely run them to earth!'

'So much for your aiyaar's craft!' said the prince. 'See how smartly I recovered the book!'

'I know how well versed you are in this art,' Tej pulled a face. 'But how did you find it? We're surrounded with wonders!'

Virendra told them how he got the book and the letter—even about his reply.

'She seems to be from a noble family. She couldn't bear to see the prince suffer,' Jagannath said. 'However, she knows everything about him, while we know nothing about her.'

'That's a matter of shame for Tej Singh,' Virendra said. 'He can't locate the whereabouts of a few women.'

'I'll find them and you'll be dumbfounded when I do it,' Tej replied. 'But now that we have the book again, we should solve the mystery of the ruins.'

'Do you think Bankanya will wait all that while?' Virendra said.

'Don't you care about Chandrakanta any longer?' Tej asked.

'That's not true. I love her as much as ever. But can't both tasks proceed side by side?'

'All right. We'll explore the ruins during the day and look for the girls at night,' Tej decided.

*

The next day they returned to their task. The book had advised that they leave the tilism three hours before the day ended. So they hurried to the courtyard where the stone man slept. Virendra measured five hands' length from the head of the platform, then began to dig the earth with his bare hands. When he had gone a yard deep, they glimpsed a white rock with an iron ring embedded in it. He removed the stone and cried out with excitement.

An underground chamber lay beneath! Tej lit a torch and they climbed down the steps.

The room was sparklingly clean. A beautiful marble image stood in the centre, with a hook in one hand and a hammer in the other. The prince took the hook and hammered it into its ear. The statue's lips began to move and music was heard, as if it were singing. After a while, it fell apart and a small rose bush, about eight fingers high, emerged from its belly. It was covered with flowers and a key hung from one of its branches. They also found a small copper plate on which was written:

This plant has been created by our esteemed Vaidya Ajaibdutt. Its flowers bear the fragrance of roses. It will spread far and never fade. Vaidyaji has left this unique plant here as a special gift to place in your court.

'What a marvel!' cried the prince. They were exclaiming over the breathtaking workmanship and sweet scent, when a door suddenly opened up on one side. Curious, they stepped out and discovered a lovely garden. It was the same garden Chapla had passed through earlier.

Following the instructions given in the book, Virendra tied the key he had found on the rose plant to a rope and began to walk around the garden, dragging the key on the ground. When he reached a fountain, the key suddenly stuck to the ground. The prince directed the others to dig that spot.

They had gone two or three hands deep, when Jagannath said, 'We should stop. It's just three hours to sunset.'

They halted work and left. On the way out the prince locked the stone trap door through which they had entered with the same key.

Outmanoeuvred!

Dusk was still a couple of hours away when Tej said, 'Up, my idle friends. Time to run those mysterious women to earth.'

The aiyaars headed for the forest. After walking a while, they saw a masked rider some distance ahead. They followed him, taking care to remain hidden behind the trees. He seemed to be headed towards Chunar, but stopped several times in between, looked back, then continued.

The sun went down, and it was hard to keep track in the dark. But they followed the crunching of the horse's hooves on the dry leaves. One hour after dusk they reached the edge of the forest. The rider dismounted. They noticed several horses tethered close by. He tied his horse there, and placed a handful of hay from a nearby pile before it.

The rider continued on foot, with the aiyaars following him for another couple of hours before reaching the banks of the Ganga. Two spots of light were reflected in the water, looking like two moons floating upon it. When they got closer, they discovered a beautifully decorated boat, carrying a bevy of lovely women. The most charming one sat on a high cushion in the centre. Lit up by the lamps glowing on either side of her, her face seemed as lustrous as the moon. They stood and watched, mesmerized.

The masked one whistled when he reached the shore. Someone whistled back from the boat. Two women rose and untied a smaller boat from the side, then rowed it to the shore and he got in.

'What a lovely sight they make!' Tej's eyes shone.

'They seem to be a group of fairies,' said the astrologer. 'Shall we swim towards the boat?'

'Be careful they don't fly away with you,' Devi smiled.

'I think they're the same women the prince saw,' Tej said.

'So it seems,' Devi nodded slowly.

'What are you scared of? Come on, let's swim there and find out.' Jagannath was eager to see the women up close.

'What use was it to bring you along if you can't divine who they are?' Devi asked in annoyance.

'How can I tell? They seem to have changed their names. Viyogini, Yogini, Bhootani, Dakini—these are the bizarre names that come up,' Jagannath fumed. 'They want to confuse us.'

'Can't you find out where they stay?' Devi asked

'When I try, water appears as their dwelling place. So—are they fish?' Jagannath frowned.

'Can't you make sure?' Tej said.

'Look—air, water, earth and fire—these elements always create problems with divination. I'll explain it to you some day. Let's swim to the boat right now.'

The aiyaars took off their clothes and left them on the shore, making sure to carry their bags with them. They had barely gone a few arm lengths when someone whistled. Immediately the lamps went out. It became pitch dark and the boat could no longer be seen.

'Go on, swim there,' Devi said to the astrologer.

'They're real tricksters!' Tej sighed.

'Well, we might as well turn back,' Devi shrugged. 'I think someone was watching us from the bank. He signalled to them.'

When they reached the shore they got another surprise. Their clothes had vanished!

'My deepest respects, Jagannathji, now we've lost our clothes too!' Devi said. 'If I could lay my hands on any of them right now, I'd swallow them alive.'

'I think they're better aiyaars than us.' Tej's mouth drooped.

'Indeed, they couldn't have done better than this,' said the astrologer, hugging his chest.

Cursing, moaning, shivering, they left for the camp. It was already past midnight.

The prince had been up all night, waiting anxiously for the aiyaars to get back. When they turned up just before dawn, naked, panting, his eyes almost popped out in shock.

'What *is* this?' he asked.

'Well, you can see what it is,' Tej said brusquely. 'We'll tell you the rest when we catch our breaths.'

They sent for a new set of clothes. By the time they got dressed, the sun had risen.

'We've been so soundly outmanoeuvred that we'll remember it for the rest of our lives,' Tej said.

'But what happened?' asked the prince.

'What happened? We found those ladies but they deliberately evaded us. Bankanya says she loves you to distraction, but why does she hide from you?' Tej glowered.

'Didn't you learn anything at all?' Virendra asked.

'We set eyes on her, that's why we were punished,' Tej replied. 'She has extraordinary aiyaars.'

'Come out with it now!' said the prince.

When Tej told him the whole story, he laughed heartily. 'Your divination has failed,' he said to the astrologer.

'What can I say, they were nothing but trouble.' Jagannath shook his head.

'Can't you find out if they have any connection with Shivdutt's aiyaars?' Virendra asked.

'None. That much I've been able to learn.'

'A small blessing,' Tej put in.

'We'll go there during the day and find out,' Devi said.

'And what about the ruins?' Tej asked.

'We can suspend that for a day,' Virendra said.

'I told you, you've forgotten Chandrakanta,' Tej looked stricken.

'No, I care more for Chandrakanta than anyone else in the world,' the prince said. 'But I'm also anxious to learn about Bankanya.'

'I have to take Badrinath to the cave too. He might just escape from here,' Tej frowned.

They decided that Tej would do that, while Devi and Jagannath tried to unravel the Bankanya mystery.

But when Tej reached the cave with Badrinath bundled on his back, he got another shock. He was unable to open the secret door!

Strange Visitors

Devi and Jagannath had gone just a short distance, when they encountered one of the masked riders.

'Where are you off to, Devi Singh?' she called out. 'You got royal treatment yesterday. Now do you want to be made captive too? If you're patient, we'll teach you how to perfect your art in a few days.'

Devi was taken aback, but all the same he turned to Jagannath and said, 'Listen to this—what can this fantastic person who hides her face in shame teach us?'

'What will the astrologer listen to? We've rendered his knowledge useless,' the rider said scornfully. 'He makes thousands of calculations and they all turn to dust.'

'If we stay here, we won't leave before finding out,' Devi said.

'Where would you go?' replied the masked one. 'You'll see us every day, but remain as ignorant as before.'

Devi slyly jumped up and pulled the mask off. But to his dismay, he found the woman's face was coloured red. He couldn't make out anything. Worse, she swiftly pulled off his turban, flung a letter at him and rode off.

It was addressed to 'Prince Virendra Singh'.

'It seems they are all accomplished aiyaars,' Jagannath said hopelessly.

Defeated once again, they returned to the camp with the letter.

The contents of the letter threw the prince into a greater state of confusion. It said:

Whatever may happen, I cannot reveal myself to you till you agree to the following conditions:

1. You agree to marry both Chandrakanta and me on the same day and at the same auspicious moment.
2. I should not be considered any less than Chandrakanta because I am her equal in all respects.

If you don't agree, I'll return home. But let me warn you, you may try for a thousand years but you will not find Chandrakanta without my help.

All this aggravated Virendra's anxiety. He was very much in love with Bankanya, but his feelings for Chandrakanta were as strong as ever. And how could he marry both at the same time? Would the princess and her father agree? But Bankanya said he could not find Chandrakanta without her help.

After some thought he decided to pen an agreement accepting all these conditions. Chandrakanta would surely understand when he explained.

Devi and the astrologer were baffled too when he showed them the letter. Virendra spent a whole day thinking of what he should write in response.

The next morning Tej returned with Badrinath, creating more bewilderment. 'The door is locked from inside,' he said. 'What could have happened?'

'Someone has either spoilt the lock or Shivdutt has done something,' Jagannath said.

'Why would he want to remain locked up?' Tej asked.

'I wonder if Bankanya is behind this,' the prince rubbed his chin.

'That's too far-fetched,' Tej said. 'What connection could she have?'

'She's written saying that I will not be able to find Chandrakanta without her help, apart from a couple of other things. I was wondering what to do,' Virendra said. 'But your experience makes me suspicious.'

'Then why did she return the book?' Tej wondered. 'Let me see the letter.'

The letter confounded Tej. Finally the prince said, 'I feel there's no harm agreeing to Bankanya's terms. If she is pleased, we'll definitely get some information.'

'Do what you feel is right,' Tej spread his hands. 'Poor

Chandrakanta won't object. But will the king agree? Who knows what Bankanya's origins are?'

'She says she's no less than the princess,' Virendra said.

Just then a sentry entered to say that there was a visitor for the prince. When Virendra nodded assent, a short, dark-complexioned man, peculiarly dressed in trousers of sacking and a cane hat, armed with a sword and shield entered.

His appearance evoked laughter, and Tej and Devi made mocking remarks, but he remained unfazed and said, 'I've come for the reply to the letter that was given to Devi and the astrologer.'

Devi was about to comment, but Tej stopped him. The visitor bowed in appreciation and said, 'Could I have the reply please? I have far to go.'

The prince wrote at the back of the same letter, 'I accept with all my heart,' and sealed it with his ring.

The same afternoon, another strange visitor was announced. It was an old woman, around seventy, with two large and dirty protruding teeth. She wore a filthy sari, a big brass ring on her nose and brass anklets.

'What do you want?' Tej asked.

'I will speak only to the prince,' she said. 'And what I say will be of great benefit to him.' She began to cough loudly.

When Tej and Devi commented, she said to Virendra, 'Promise that no one will interrupt or harass or imprison me.'

'Why would I do that, if you tell me something which will be of help to me?' the prince replied.

'I'm afraid because I have accomplished something your aiyaars could not in a thousand years. I can tell you all about Bankanya. Also how to get Chandrakanta out of the tilism in just one minute,' she said.

That pleased them all. 'So tell us quickly,' said the prince.

'First tell me what reward you will give me.'

'Whatever you ask, provided what you say is true,' Virendra said.

'Promise me first.'

'Let me know what you want, before I promise.'

'All I ask is that you should marry me. I don't care when you marry Chandrakanta and Bankanya but you'll have to marry me today. I've been in love with you for a long time and grown old waiting for you,' the hag said. 'Now don't delay or you'll be sorry.'

Virendra almost choked with shock. His face burned with rage. Tej ground his teeth, Devi clenched his fists and Jagannath cursed below his breath. But they would not act unless the prince ordered them. Else they would have torn the old woman apart.

'Is she an aiyaar or does she actually look like this?' Tej asked the astrologer.

Jagannath put a hand on his nose and used his breath to discern the truth. 'She is not an aiyaar.'

'Get out immediately!' Tej cried. 'Or we won't be able to control ourselves. To think such witches can fancy themselves in love with the prince!'

'You'll be sorry.' The old woman glared at him with reddened eyes. 'I locked your cave prison and you couldn't get in. Now I'll go and set Shivdutt free. See what a tussle I'll generate.'

She hobbled out.

'She will give us trouble,' Virendra said. 'She claims she locked up your cave prison Tej.'

'I can't figure it out,' Tej scratched his head. 'But we'll only know if Shivdutt gets out.'

'Oh, that I had to see this day,' sighed the prince.

'Please don't worry,' Tej said. 'Devi has gone after her.'

'There's a jinx on your art!' the prince said angrily. 'Bankanya or the old woman, it's the same old story.'

The words pierced Tej and the astrologer through and through, but they left the tent silently.

*

Devi followed the woman. She tramped on and on. When night fell, she reached a small row of hills and entered a cave so narrow that only one person could go in at a time.

Assuming it might be her home Devi waited outside under a tree. He sat there all night, but she did not come out even once. So, when dawn broke, he went inside. He found that the cave was actually a tunnel. It was pitch dark inside. He must have walked two miles, groping his way, when he glimpsed some light. He stepped out to find himself near a stream with a dense forest all around. The old woman had outwitted him! Fuming, disheartened, he returned through the tunnel. It was too risky to try some other route back to camp.

When he reached, he found several men sitting with the prince, along with Fateh Singh.

'So what did you discover?' Virendra asked.

'She fooled me well and proper,' Devi said and narrated his misadventure.

Virendra's face fell.

'But where's my guru? And the astrologer?' Devi asked Fateh.

'Tej went off in a rage, along with the astrologer. The prince told him that his art was on the decline,' Fateh said.

'That means he'll come back with some results,' Devi looked pleased.

'We'll see.' The prince's mouth curled.

That very moment Tej and Jagannath entered, their faces wreathed with smiles.

'What's the news?' Virendra asked.

'It's good. But I won't tell you now,' Tej replied.

'Won't you tell me, guruji?' Devi said.

'I should tell you because you acknowledge me as your teacher?' Tej laughed. 'What great deeds did you perform today?'

'I disgraced you as a pupil.' Devi hung his head.

Just then a sentry entered and said with a bow, 'Maharaja Shivdutt's prime minister is here.'

The prince exchanged a glance with Tej, then said, 'He can come in, but alone.'

The minister entered. He bowed and uncovered a salver heaped with gleaming jewels. 'I've brought these as tribute from Maharaja Shivdutt. By God's grace and your kindness, he has been set free and acknowledges you as his overlord. He has sent a letter too. Please accept this offering.'

The prince nodded in agreement and handed the salver to Tej. The minister was asked to sit down and Virendra's retinue summoned since he wished to hold court. When the place had filled up, Tej Singh read out the letter:

I was released from the cave prison in a manner which I can only acknowledge as the result of your mercy. You must be wondering how this happened, but I cannot disclose the details right now or pay my respects personally. The truth will be revealed when the right moment arrives. All I hope for now is your forgiveness. Please accept my gift. From this day on neither my servants nor my aiyaars will harass yours, and I expect the same from you.

Yours,
Shivdutt.

Everyone nodded approval. The prince immediately ordered that Badrinath be set free and handed over to the Chunar prime minister. He invited them to enjoy his hospitality for a couple of days more.

When the others had left, Virendra and Fateh sat and discussed this strange development with the aiyaars in private.

'Tej, the old woman did accomplish what she threatened,' the prince said, frowning.

'But Shivdutt's letter says something quite different,' Tej answered.

'Can we trust him?' Devi said.

'My predictions tell me that he wrote the truth. But who knows what he'll do later?' asked the astrologer.

'If it's the truth, why didn't he tell us how he got free?' Tej mused.

They puzzled over the matter for a long while but could not come to any conclusion.

*

The next morning they were back at the ruins, digging at the same place. They had gone eight to nine hands deep when they came upon what looked like the lid of a chest. It was locked and the keyhole plugged with a stone to protect it.

The prince wanted to pull the chest out but it turned out to be an impossible task. The chest seemed to be incredibly large. Even after digging up a large area they could not locate the sides.

Confounded, Virendra consulted the book again. It said:

Tie the key to a rope and drag it on the ground again till it sticks. Dig at that spot till the top of the chest emerges. It is not really a chest but a door. Then dig at a distance of seven hands to the east from the fountain in the centre of the garden. You will find a mud pot there with a key inside it. This key will unlock that door.

It leads to a dark underground chamber full of smoke. Do not attempt to light a torch here or this vapour will burst into flames. Wrap your faces carefully so the smoke does not go to your heads. You will shortly arrive at a brightly lit chamber. It is full of wires stretching from the roof to the ground. Cut them away with your swords, then come out.

Following these instructions, they reached the room. But despite taking precautions the smoke made them feel light-headed. Hurriedly, they scrambled out and collapsed on the ground. When they came to their senses, they found that two hours had elapsed and very little time remained, so they left.

In the evening, as usual, the prince wanted to roam the forest. As they were strolling along, they found a piece of paper stuck to a tree.

Devi went to read it.

Now you know the kind of problems I can create. I told you that if you marry me, I'll help you solve the mystery in just an hour and release Chandrakanta. You didn't, so I set Shivdutt free. Will you marry me now? If you're willing, place your reply in this same place. If you don't agree, I'll finish both Chandrakanta and Chapla off. You know how I outsmarted Devi Singh. I also persuaded Shivdutt to make peace with you. So . . . think before you act!

Yours,
Surajmukhi.

Devi beckoned to the others to read it. When they came to the name 'Surajmukhi', they burst out laughing.

'Whatever she may claim, she cannot harm the prince in

any way,' Jagannath said.

But Virendra said morosely, 'She has already proved true to her word.'

They came across several other such letters stuck to trees in the forest. Overwhelmed with gloom, the prince returned to the camp.

After dinner, the aiyaars left on their night rounds while Virendra lay on his bed, battling his worries.

Then he heard a footstep. It was Tej.

'We've discovered something interesting,' he said.

'What is it?' Virendra started up and followed him.

A crowd had gathered outside the camp. The moment the men saw the prince, they stepped aside.

Krur Singh's body lay on the ground, clearly visible in the light from their torches. He was covered with blood and a dagger was thrust in his belly.

'So, you finally killed him, Tej!' the prince exclaimed.

'Do we aiyaars kill in this manner?' Tej frowned.

'Then who did?'

'I have no idea. We noticed three or four men loitering behind the ruins. They fled as soon as they saw us. When we went closer, we found Krur lying there. Devi rushed back and arranged for a palanquin and some bearers to carry him. He has not expired as yet, but is not likely to survive.'

'That's strange,' the prince frowned. 'Why don't you remove the dagger?'

Tej pulled out the dagger, washed it and took it to Virendra. When they examined it, they found something engraved on the hilt. It was Chapla's name!

'Chapla!' Tej cried out. 'I recognize this dagger. It was always tied to her waist. But how did it get here? Did she kill Krur?'

'Poor Chapla must be sitting in that dark cave with the princess,' Devi said.

'Then how did her dagger get here?' Virendra asked.

'And why did Krur come here?' Tej said. 'He had joined Shivdutt.'

The Chunar prime minister was called. When he saw Krur, he said, 'The wretch has got the punishment he deserved. The day his majesty was set free, he proclaimed that none of his followers should do anything to harm Prince Virendra. After that Krur, Nazim and Ahmed all disappeared with their families.'

Even as they watched, Krur Singh hiccupped a few times and gave up the ghost.

'Dispose of his body, Tej, and keep the dagger,' the prince said.

Tej had the corpse removed and they went back to their tents.

An Amazing Discovery

But the ruins awaited them, so in the morning they got back to work.

The book said:

Once the wires are cut, after a while the smoke will disperse. A square red stone is placed on the marble throne that lies in the black stone pavilion. Anyone who touches it will fall down unconscious. But by cutting the wires you will prevent that. The underground chamber lies beneath the pavilion and the wires are attached to the throne at the top and placed in many kinds of chemicals at the bottom. Light torches and enter the chamber. You will find a vast treasure there. Take as much as you want, and do not proceed further into the ruins till you have removed the

treasure. Take the red stone, too. It is actually a small box with
several useful objects inside it. You will find the keys in the ruins.

The prince went through the instructions once more, and felt ready to go ahead. They lit torches and found the slashed wires scattered everywhere. The chamber was simply enormous. Hundreds of iron and silver trunks lay all around, and a bunch of keys hung from a peg on the wall.

Virendra took the keys and opened one box. Fabulous diamond ornaments winked up at him. He closed it and opened another. It was full of swords and daggers, their ornate hilts studded with even larger diamonds.

'What a find!' the prince cried breathlessly. He turned to Tej. 'There's no point opening all the boxes now. We should open them one by one and send them to Naugarh right away.'

'If you open all, it'll take you at least ten days to go through them,' Tej said. 'We will not be able to work our way through the ruins. You should send them off unopened. That way no one will learn about the treasure. I'm certain someone built this maze deliberately, to protect this vast fortune.'

The idea appealed to the prince and Devi and the astrologer agreed too. After locking the door to the underground chamber, they left. The prince handed over the bunch of keys to Tej, saying, 'Now you take charge and dispatch all the boxes to Naugarh.'

The task took several days. Tej had to arrange for transport as well as guards to ensure that no one tried to loot the treasure. That meant the business of penetrating the maze came to a halt.

Virendra's Midnight Adventure

One night, after tossing and turning on his bed as usual, the prince fell into a deep sleep. He awoke, and found that instead of his tent, he was lying in a richly furnished room!

Ornate chandeliers hung from the ceiling and the marble walls were covered with pictures of lovely women. The finely wrought doors were shut and candles still glowed in the alcoves. His gaze sped past all the pictures to rest on a large life-sized one, framed in gold.

'How gorgeous!' he exclaimed. 'It's the best among them . . . definitely. And . . . oh . . . it's—it's my beloved's portrait!'

Leaping from the bed, he went to examine it. 'Those large

eyes, how amazingly rendered,' he mused. 'The pink of her cheeks, the smile on her finely wrought lips, her earrings, bindi and nose ring . . . how exquisitely her necklace has been painted! The gleaming rubies, the setting—with what artistry! Her bracelets, rings—all so lifelike! And look at Chapla and Champa posing beside her with fingers on their chins . . . Ah, where could my Chandrakanta be!'

The jingle of an anklet made him start. There were several small windows with glass panes in the room; but they were all closed. Where did the sound come from? Who was the woman?

He had shaken off his torpor now and began to wonder how he had arrived here. Was it a dream? He returned to the bed and lay down, but remained wide awake. Suddenly he heard the anklet again. He went straight to the doors and pushed them hard. All seven of them opened up easily.

A lush garden lay outside and Virendra realized that it must be at least three hours past daybreak. The place was overgrown with wild flowers and creepers. There was a small tank in the middle and neatly crafted stairs led into it. Two large jamun trees shaded it, their trunks enclosed with marble platforms. A fine rug was spread on the platform on the left and a silver pot with a spout placed next to it, along with a neem twig all prepared for cleaning teeth. A dhoti, shoulder cloth and other richly fashioned garments lay on a small silver stool.

On the platform on the right, all the articles needed for worship were set on another silver stool. Little jewelled bowls, a soft woollen prayer rug and even a bel fruit to offer.

The prince was even more puzzled. Then he noticed a paper attached to the tree trunk. 'Prince Virendra Singh, all these things are for your use. Today you are our guest,' it said.

What fine arrangements, the prince thought. Surely fairies brought me here. But I can't see anyone! He decided to explore the place before bathing.

He noticed another room next to the one he had woken up in, but the doors were tightly shut. He gave up and got dressed, then performed his puja. The sun was very strong now, so he tried to go inside, but could not enter the first room. However, the doors of the second one opened mysteriously.

A fine Kashmiri carpet was spread on the marble floor and a vast array of sumptuous food set out in dishes of gold and silver. He discovered another note. 'Do not be afraid. This house belongs to a friend of yours and you are a most honoured guest. Please enjoy the meal.'

Virendra did not wish to eat before he learnt who his host was. But hunger overpowered him, so he stretched out a hand, then drew it back again.

The sound of laughter startled him. He glanced around, looked up at the windows but there was no one there. Then a voice said, 'Please go ahead and eat. It is quite safe.'

The prince was starving by now, so he finished the meal, washed his hands and lay down on the bed nearby. Within minutes he was fast asleep.

He awoke to the sound of music and found himself in a beautifully decorated pavilion instead of the room. It was quite dark now, but the place was brightly lit. It seemed to be another garden, full of large trees. Several charming women were strolling around, singing and playing musical instruments. Occasionally, they would stop to chat and exchange a laugh. Intrigued, the prince rose and approached them cautiously.

The women stopped to stare at him, puzzled. One came forward.

'Who are you?' she asked. 'And why did you enter the garden without permission?'

She was extremely pretty and lively looking. 'I don't know whose garden this is,' Virendra replied. 'Can you tell me?'

'First answer my question, then I'll answer yours,' said the woman.

'I don't know why and how I came here.'

'Wonderful! What an innocent thief,' the woman said, turning to the others.

The women surrounded him, and a volley of remarks came his way.

'Tell us the truth.'

'Search him, he's definitely stolen something!'

'Look at the way he's dressed—like a prince!'

'From where did you steal those clothes?'

The prince was completely baffled. After a while, he said, 'It looks like you people brought me here.'

'Why would we bring you here? What can you do for us? You definitely came here to make off with something,' one said.

'All right, show me the way out, and I'll leave,' the prince said, harassed.

'Look at him! He says he doesn't know the way,' another said.

'He wants to fool us and escape,' remarked a third.

'We should arrest him,' shouted a fourth one.

'Where will you take me?' the prince asked.

'To our mistress.'

'What's her name?'

'How dare you ask! If anyone takes her name, his or her tongue will fall out.'

'Then how do you converse with her? And how do you tell people whom you serve?'

'We speak only to her picture and carry a small portrait around our necks. That's how people know whom we serve,' another said.

'Will you show it to me?' Virendra asked.

'Here!' One held up the small picture hanging on her neck.

The prince was stunned. It was Chandrakanta! But Chandrakanta was the princess of Vijaygarh!

'What's the name of this city?' he asked.

'Chitranagar, because everyone carries the princess's picture. It has had this name for thousands of years. I inherited this picture from my great-grandmother,' one of the girls said.

'But who are her parents? And since when has she ruled this city?'

'We don't know! We present ourselves before a large picture of hers, which can speak. It gives us our orders.'

'Your talk is driving me crazy,' Virendra said. 'Can you take me to that picture?'

'We have to arrest you and take you there, in any case.'

'But what have I done? And if a picture is your mistress, how have I wronged it?'

'Our princess remains hidden from sight. She sees everything. She has been doing this for thousands of years and will continue to do so.'

'Stop giving him explanations,' one of the women said. 'He's trying to evade his punishment.'

'He seems to be of noble birth,' said the first. 'We should treat him politely.'

'And, pray, who are you and who's your father?' the third asked, looking sceptical.

'I'm Virendra Singh, the son of Maharaja Surendra Singh of Naugarh.'

The women looked delighted. 'We must arrest him,' one said. 'He's the one who broke into the mystery house and stole the royal treasure. We'll receive a handsome reward. Tie him up right away!'

The prince was utterly confounded. He swung between perplexity, astonishment and fear. Finally he said, 'All right, take me to your princess. There's no need to get aggressive. I'll go willingly.'

'Then we don't need make any fuss,' one said.

There were nine women. One went ahead to inform the

court, while four walked in front of him and four guarded him from behind.

They went to a corner of the garden and a small door opened in the walls, leading into a well-decorated garden, brightly lit. Macebearers roamed about, carrying gold and silver staffs, along with many other people.

No one spoke to the women or questioned them. They walked boldly into a large court, so magnificent and richly decked that the prince was wonderstruck.

His gaze fell on the portrait placed on a throne. It seemed to be of Chandrakanta, with a crown on her head and a canopy shading her. Two lions were seated on either side of the throne. They kept growling and snarling. Lavishly costumed courtiers sat silently in two rows before the throne, their heads bowed.

The splendour of the court, along with the presence of Chandrakanta's picture, overwhelmed the prince. He stood there unable to speak.

Then a voice came from behind the picture. 'Who is this?'

'We caught him roaming in the royal garden,' one woman said. 'On enquiring we learnt that he's the same Virendra Singh who has entered the imperial maze.'

'If it is true, take him away and keep him under watch, while we decide what to do with him!' the voice said.

The women took Virendra to another luxuriously furnished room. He was utterly confounded now. It was impossible to figure out all that he had seen and experienced. Two hours went by while he sat there, wondering what was going on. Then overcome with thirst, he looked for water. Instantly, a girl appeared and offered him a drink from a golden bowl. After drinking the water he felt calmer and sleep overcame him.

*

Meanwhile, back at the camp, when the prince was found missing, there was a huge outcry. Tej and Devi scurried here and there searching for him. By evening the astrologer said he had divined Virendra's whereabouts.

'A group of women abducted him after rendering him unconscious. He is locked up in a house in the Naugarh region. That's all I've found.'

'Naugarh is his own kingdom,' Tej said. 'The public is loyal and devoted. How could he have any enemies there? Let's investigate.'

Leaving the book of mystery in safekeeping with Fateh Singh, the three aiyaars set off. When they had walked for about ten miles in the forest, the sun started to rise, so they disguised themselves and went on, not stopping to eat or drink. They had decided that they would search for the prince without informing anyone. But though they scoured the city through and through, they could not find any clue.

The next day they attended the court in disguise. As they stood there, a spy entered and approached the prime minister Jeet Singh.

'Your honour,' he said, in a voice full of panic, 'our beloved

Prince Virendra has vanished and the aiyaars have failed to locate him. But Jagannath the astrologer has divined that he is hidden in Naugarh.'

'But we have no enemies here!' Jeet Singh frowned.

'There's worse news,' the spy continued. 'The moment the aiyaars left, Shivdutt attacked the camp, wounded Fateh Singh and took him prisoner. This left our forces in disarray.'

Maharaja Surendra Singh's brow darkened with rage. 'Prepare our remaining troops for battle. I'll teach that scoundrel a thing or two!' he said.

The prime minister was about to reply, when two other spies arrived. 'Your majesty, Maharaja Jai Singh heard what had happened and set out for Chunar with his army. On the way he learnt that Shivdutt disappeared mysteriously, the very night he captured Fateh Singh. Fateh is now free, he has returned to the camp and our forces are regrouping.'

'Let us leave for Chunar right away, and finish this business once and for all,' said the king, rising.

The aiyaars did not stop any longer. They found a quiet place and began to plan their strategy. Finally Tej agreed to the astrologer's suggestion that they visit the cave prison, even though he had misgivings about being able to open the door again. However, when they got there, they had no problems at all, luckily.

*

The prince had slipped on to the mattress, unconscious.

When he awoke he found himself lying on a rock! Disconcerted, he gazed about him. Tall hills all around, a stream gurgling in between, jamun trees clustering on its banks—it looked just like the place where Tej locked up his captives.

Agitated, he got up and began to explore his surroundings. He found much that was familiar. And when he saw Shivdutt reclining on a rock and his faithful wife massaging his feet, his doubts vanished. The two were facing the other way so they did not notice Virendra.

The prince rushed to the spot from where he had last glimpsed Chandrakanta and Chapla. They were still there. The princess was in the same piteous state, in a torn, soiled sari, dishevelled, with her hair tangled and uncombed.

The moment he set eyes on her, his love overpowered him. Tears came to his eyes. Ashamed, he concealed himself behind a tree. I cannot face her, he thought. How can I tell her that I haven't yet managed to penetrate the maze? That my infatuation for Bankanya deflected me from my purpose? He was surprised to see Shivdutt there, though. Hadn't his prime minister himself brought the news that he'd been set free?

The Mystery Thickens

All this was whirling in his mind when he caught sight of Tej. Devi and Jagannath followed close behind. The moment Tej set eyes on the prince, he ran and fell at his feet. Virendra embraced him and greeted the others joyfully.

The three sat down under a tree to talk. 'Tej,' said the prince. 'Look, Chandrakanta is sitting there, dressed in torn clothes, as dejected as when we saw her last. Chapla is trying to wipe her face with her sari.'

'Didn't you speak to her?' Tej asked.

'No.' The prince hung his head. 'I wondered if I should show myself.'

'For how many days have you been trying to make up your mind?'

'I arrived here barely a few moments ago,' said the prince.

'What?' Tej was astonished. 'Where have you been all these days? I thought that your passion overcame you, and you stole here to gaze at the princess.'

'I didn't leave on my own. Someone carried me away from the camp,' the prince said.

'You haven't learned who it was yet?' Tej was even more surprised.

'No. I couldn't.'

Virendra then gave them an account of his adventures. The aiyaars listened wide-eyed.

'What do you make of this?' Tej asked the astrologer.

'I am as much in the dark.' Jagannath shook his head.

'The wonders I experienced in the last two-three days were far greater than any we encountered while trying to find our way through the ruins,' Virendra said.

'A weak-hearted man would have died of fright,' Devi observed.

'Something even more amazing,' Virendra said. 'Shivdutt is here—under the shade of those trees.'

'That's really strange!' Tej said. 'Let's find out how he returned.'

'Chandrakanta's there on the hill just above him,' said the prince. 'We should inquire how she is first. But if she asks what I've been doing, I won't know what to say!'

'Well, lovers are invariably reduced to this state,' Tej smirked. 'Don't worry. I'll speak on your behalf.'

Chapla noticed them first.

She rose and said, 'I hope you are well, Prince Virendra.'

'I'm all right. But how is Chandrakanta?

'You can see for yourself,' Chapla replied.

Chandrakanta, who was sitting there with her head bowed, started up when she heard Chapla calling out. And when she saw the prince, she folded her hands and began to weep.

'Please . . . be patient for a while longer,' Virendra said. 'I have managed to break through a portion of the maze. I had to come here . . . for various reasons. I-I'll return to the task now.'

'The princess says her heart is full of foreboding. Either your love has waned, or someone else has replaced her in your affections,' Chapla replied. 'I've been suffering for a long time because of this unexpected calamity, she says. But this new fear torments me far, far more.'

Tej smiled. 'Shall I let the cat out of the bag?' he said to the prince.

Tears fell from Virendra's eyes. Speechless, he folded his hands and gazed at the princess.

Tej playfully pulled his hands apart. 'Can't you see how your words have affected him?' he told Chapla. 'Please tell the princess that she doesn't need to fear anything.'

'But why did you come here today?' Chapla asked.

'We came to check on Shivdutt,' Tej said. 'We heard that he'd been set free.'

'It must be an aiyaar posing as him,' Chapla said. 'These two have been here all along.'

'Let me talk to him,' Tej said.

Shivdutt had been listening to their conversation. He approached the prince and was about to say something when he looked up and saw Chandrakanta and Chapla. He halted immediately.

'Go ahead, why did you stop?' Tej asked.

'I cannot tell you anything,' Shivdutt replied.

'Why?'

'My life is at risk.'

'Who'll harm you if you do?'

'If I tell you, the secret will be out.'

'If you don't, I won't spare you either,' Tej frowned.

'Do what you will,' Shivdutt shrugged.

Tej drew his dagger, but Chapla cried out, 'Don't! Don't do that!'

Tej looked up. 'Why are you attacking him?' Chapla asked.

'He was about to tell me something when he looked at you and fell silent,' Tej said. 'Now he says his life is at risk if he does. As it is we are completely baffled about what happened to him. All this secrecy is driving me crazy!'

'He seems to have lost his mind,' Chapla replied. 'I've seen him shouting and racing up and down like a lunatic.'

'*She's* calling me mad?' Shivdutt glared at her.

'What did you say?' Tej asked.

'Nothing. Talk to her. I'm mad,' Shivdutt said.

'Just look at the lunatic!' Devi smirked.

'Jagannathji, please tell us something about this new kind of lunatic,' Virendra begged.

'When it's been proclaimed from above, what can I say?' Jagannath laughed.

'There's something behind this too,' Tej said. 'Well, we'll just have to wait for this mystery to unfold.'

'Someone knows it all,' Devi smiled. 'But she won't tell us.'

'We should return to the camp now,' Tej said irritably. 'But there's something I have to tell you.'

He informed the prince about the latest turn of events—the so-called Shivdutt's assault on the camp, his strange disappearance and Maharaja Jai Singh and Surendra Singh's attack on Chunar.

After the prince had reassured Chandrakanta that she would be set free soon, they left.

The Beat of Victory

Dusk had fallen when they left the cave. Devi was deputed to fetch a fine horse from the Naugarh stables without letting anyone know.

They spent the night in the forest and headed towards the camp in the morning. Suddenly they encountered a masked horseman. The moment they got close, the person dismounted, placed something on the ground, then moved away some distance.

The prince went to see what it was. 'What am I to do Tej?' he called out. 'Bankanya is loading me with obligations. Here's the book again . . . and a letter. Her love is rendering me useless.'

He read the letter aloud: 'The book of mystery had fallen

into my hands again. Take it and set Chandrakanta free. She must be very troubled. A battle is being fought in Chunar too. Go, claim the victory and thus prove your mettle.'

'Is she human, or a celestial maiden, an apsara?' Tej asked. 'She manages to accomplish all kinds of extraordinary deeds.'

'If there were just one problem to solve, how simple it would be!' The prince sighed.

'I suggest you remain here while I find out what's going on at Chunar,' Devi said.

Virendra had to waste another day, waiting.

Devi returned and told them, 'The Chunar aiyaars had abducted Maharaja Jai Singh, but Jeet Singh entered the fort in disguise and set him free. He outwitted Badrinath and captured him, along with Pannalal, Ramnarayan and Chunnilal. The battle is still raging. Our forces have reached the city gates but are unable to break them down. The enemy's cannons are wreaking havoc.'

'If we could get inside the fort somehow and open the gates,' Virendra's brow furrowed, 'it would be an act of great daring.'

'Yes, let us try!' Tej's eyes gleamed. 'We might succeed. If not . . . we'll just lose our lives.'

'Either way we'll attain glory,' said the prince, 'by conquering Chunar or achieving martyrdom.'

The idea appealed to all of them and they decided to try and scale the walls at night and open the gates in the morning.

'When the battle is at its height,' Virendra said, 'and most of their soldiers are up on the walls repelling the attack, it won't be difficult to steal in among the fifty or hundred men at the gate and force them open.'

They reached Chunar that very night. Then disguising themselves, they seized an opportunity, threw ropes over the walls and climbed up.

*

It was three hours after daybreak. Fateh Singh's army had made a determined onslaught and reached the gates of the fort. The Chunar forces were bombarding them from the walls, trying their best to throw them back. All of a sudden the gates parted and four yellow flags flashed defiantly. This was the colour of Virendra's emblem. Maharaja Surendra Singh, Jai Singh, the whole army saw the flags clearly. Elated, not stopping to figure out what had happened, Fateh Singh burst in. His warriors overran the fort and subdued the defenders with ease. Fateh Singh slashed down Shivdutt's green pennant and replaced it with Virendra Singh's yellow one. Then he picked up the drum that lay below the flag and struck it thrice with the stick—'Kroom-dhoom-fateh!', the beat of victory. The Chunar army knew their cause was lost and surrendered.

The prince had cut down forty men with his own hands, but was severely wounded, as were the aiyaars. They were still in disguise. His father had barely entered when he fell at his feet along with the others, still bearing their flags.

Jeet Singh attended to them right away, washing and

bandaging their wounds. Only after their faces were washed were their real identities revealed.

Surendra Singh embraced his son joyfully, Jai Singh blessed him and the kingdom sang their praises. There was rejoicing all around.

Now that Chunar was theirs, the two kings jointly placed Virendra on the throne and crowned him that very day. Lavish gifts were distributed to all the soldiers and the celebrations continued for a week. Shivdutt's followers vowed allegiance to the prince.

After leaving adequate forces in Chunar, Surendra Singh and Jai Singh left for their respective kingdoms and exhorted Virendra to complete the task of penetrating the maze of mystery.

More Obstacles

Two portions of the tilism remained to be broken through. One was the platform on which the stone man slept and the second was the python door, which led to the place where Chandrakanta and Chapla were trapped.

There were no instructions for entering the first part. The book said:

This platform is the door to another maze, even more complicated than this one. It is full of unbelievable treasures and the most extraordinary marvels. The method of entry is different and the key lies with the stone man.

'Tell me, Jagannathji, will I be able to unlock this maze?' Virendra asked.

'We'll see,' said the astrologer. 'First set the princess free.'

The four retraced their steps and reached the garden of the treasure and the pavilion on which they had found the red stone. Then after diving into the water channel, they arrived at the courtyard where Chapla had been swallowed by the stone python.

Following the instructions in the book, the prince kicked the big black stone mounted on one of the walls. It swung open like a door and they found stairs leading down. They lit torches and entered, pausing to observe the mechanism inside the python. It consisted of several wheels, ratchets and a thick birch bark fan. Virendra figured that when anyone stepped on the stone in front of the python, the mill turned and drew the person into the python with the force of its pull. Then they discovered a small window, which they climbed through, and came to a tunnel. According to the book, this tunnel led to the courtyard where the two girls were trapped.

The prince's heart began to pound in anticipation. He glanced at Tej, who was trembling at the thought of meeting Chapla, and all of them pressed on joyfully.

I'll meet Chandrakanta in private for the first time after a long while, Virendra thought. I'll wipe her face with my own shoulder cloth, comb her tangled locks with my fingers. But he hadn't thought of bringing new clothes for her. Would she be annoyed? No, she loved him too much. He would give her his dhoti to wear and wrap his shoulder cloth about his own waist.

The sound of footsteps startled him. Were the girls coming to receive them? But how could they know they were on their way? Then he froze. Were those wolves growling? Virendra's legs turned wooden. Chill with apprehension, he went on. Somehow, he reached the courtyard.

Chandrakanta and Chapla should have been there . . . But all they found were two badly mauled corpses—so badly gnawed that only the bones were visible.

The prince began to wail. 'Who did this to you, Chandrakanta? Those cruel wolves? Or have I reached some other place? No, that wicked Shivdutt stands there below me. Ah-h, how can I live without you? I'll abandon all three of my kingdoms and join you.'

Virendra was about to leap off the edge of the hill, when one of the courtyard walls opened with a loud bang. An old man burst out and grasped his hand.

He must have been around eighty. A long beard, white as cotton wool, hung to his navel. His matted locks streamed to the ground and his body was smeared with ash. With his large red eyes and the trident in his right hand, he looked like an angry Shiva.

His whole body trembled with rage as his voice sliced through the air, 'Don't you dare try to widow anyone!'

The house seemed to shake and the three aiyaars were terror-struck. The prince was jerked back to his senses.

He gazed at the ascetic for a long time, then said, 'I thought you were Lord Shiva himself, or a holy sage, come to bless me. But you prevented me from fulfilling my dharma as a kshatriya, from taking my own life. Now I'll fight you one-handed so your trident can slay me. But why is a holy man like you uttering an untruth? Whom have I married? Whom will I widow? Oh, if poor Chandrakanta were here she might think it to be true!'

'So I'm a liar?' the sage said sternly. 'And is this a kshatriya's dharma? To forget promises? Didn't you promise to marry someone? Here, read this!'

He pulled out a letter from his matted hair. The prince started. It was the letter he'd written to Bankanya, promising to marry her. But how did the sage get hold of it?

For a moment Virendra remained silent. Then he asked, 'Do you know Bankanya?'

'Know?' the holy man said in the same harsh tone. 'I can produce her if you wish!'

He kicked the ground. It parted. Bankanya emerged and caught hold of the prince's feet!

Virendra was thunderstruck. He could not speak for a long time, wondering how Bankanya had appeared, who the sage was and why he was helping her.

Finally he said, 'I'm deeply obligated to Bankanya, but I cannot fulfil my promise without finding Chandrakanta. See—she has made a condition! How can I fulfil it when Chandrakanta is no more?'

The sage looked at Bankanya and said, 'Are you turning me into a liar?'

The girl folded her hands. 'How can I do that, sire? Please ask him why he claims Chandrakanta is dead.'

The sage turned to Virendra. 'Did you hear that? What makes you think Chandrakanta is dead?'

'When I first entered the cave, I saw Chandrakanta and Chapla here, even spoke to them. But today . . . these corpses . . . ' The prince's throat clogged up and he couldn't speak.

The sage glared at Tej now. 'Have you taken leave of your senses too? Can't you notice the difference between a woman's body and a man's?'

Tej gasped. He looked hard at the corpses again, flushed and hung his head. 'You're right. They're men's bodies. I got carried away, too.'

'A great shame for an aiyaar!' the sage glowered. 'Your mistake could have cost the prince his life. Now observe what lies between those hills! Your guru has already informed you about the underground chamber.'

Tej gazed at the spot the old man was pointing to. The prince, Devi and the astrologer followed suit.

'What is this, what has happened?' Tej suddenly exclaimed.

The others stared even harder, puzzled by his remark. Tej turned to question the sage.

But the old man had gone. So had Bankanya! The passage that had opened in the ground had closed. Only a faint crack indicated that it had ever been there!

When they recovered from the shock, Virendra said, 'What was the sage pointing to? What was it that held your attention so completely? And where have they gone?'

'How do I know where they've gone?' Tej said. 'It'll take a lot of thought to figure that out.'

'But what were you gazing at?'

'It's hard to explain now,' Tej replied. 'Let's get out of here—the stench of the dead bodies is overpowering. But before we leave, take another look at that spot between the hills. There's a door there. It's open—but it was closed earlier. That's what startled me.'

'All right,' said the prince. 'But I can't wait to hear about it.'

However, when they reached the camp at midnight, Tej told the prince, 'Go to bed now. I'll tell you everything tomorrow.'

Where is Chandrakanta?

The questions whirling around Virendra's head wouldn't let him rest. If Chandrakanta was alive, where was she? Who was Bankanya and from where did the sage appear? What had he showed Tej?

Just before daybreak, he arose and shook Tej awake. Tej well knew why. Still, he salaamed the prince politely and asked, 'What's the matter? Why are you up so early?'

'I couldn't sleep a wink,' Virendra said. 'Tell me at once—whatever you know.'

'Well, I don't know who took Chandrakanta away,' Tej said. 'Nor do I know who the sage is, and why he's helping Bankanya. But if you recall, when I first brought you to the grotto I told you that my guru had told me there were many wonders within it.'

'Yes, you said we would try to discover them some day,' Virendra said.

'My guruji said that there was a great treasure there and a small maze which could be penetrated quite easily. He had disclosed the method to me.'

'Oh . . . is that so?'

'Remember the door between the hills?' Tej continued. 'When the sage pointed to it, I noticed it was open. It struck me that someone might have broken into the maze and seized the treasure. I thought the sage might be indicating that the same person had taken Chandrakanta away. While I was trying to figure it all out, he vanished.'

Tej's words threw the prince into despair. He remained silent for a long time. Then pulling himself together, he said, 'You think this means Chandrakanta is caught in another trap?'

'It seems so.'

'How do we find out? What should we do?'

'Let's return to the cave and check out the tilism. We might find some clues,' Tej said.

'All right,' said the prince. 'But something else just came to my mind. When you went to put Badrinath there, the door wouldn't open. The same person might have locked it from inside.'

'You're right,' Tej said. 'And the same person must have set Shivdutt free.'

'And it's possible when Shivdutt decided to attack our

camp in my absence, this person captured him and locked him up again,' Virendra said.

'It is possible,' Tej said slowly.

'Which means that he's our friend,' Virendra smiled. 'But if he's our friend—why did he take Chandrakanta away?'

'This is what I can't understand.' Tej scratched his head. 'The only time we visited the cave after that was when we went looking for you. Chapla didn't mention that anyone else had been there. She said Shivdutt had been present all along and didn't seem to think they were in danger.'

'It is very complicated.' Virendra scratched his chin. 'But you made a big mistake.'

'What did I do?'

'The sage appeared from the wall. Then he kicked the ground and Bankanya emerged,' said the prince. 'He's not a god to be able to perform miracles. When they vanished, you should have kicked that spot to see if the earth might open up again. Then we'd have discovered where Bankanya came from.'

'You're right.' Tej nodded ruefully. 'What should we do now?'

'Let's go back and find out.'

The three aiyaars followed the prince through the ruins again. But when they arrived at the courtyard, they found the bodies gone. The ground looked freshly washed. Baffled, they stood there for a while. Then Tej got moving. He found the crack and kicked it hard.

The earth parted immediately and a small flight of stairs

opened up. Excited, they clambered down and found themselves in a dark room. But there was no door leading out from it, so disappointed, they had to go back. And now, no matter how hard they tried, they could not close the gap in the ground again.

'There must be a method to close it from inside,' Tej said. 'But it's escaped us. We'll just have to enter the cave from outside.'

They left the ruins and Tej secured the entrance with the same lock.

Virendra decided to go to Naugarh and meet his parents. When he got there, Jeet Singh asked the prince in private about the progress they had made. When he heard where they stood, he summoned Tej.

'Go to the cave and help the prince conquer the maze your guru told you about,' he said. 'But before that you must remove Shivdutt and his queen. Take some soldiers and send them here under guard.'

The next morning the prince reached the cave with the aiyaars. They saw Shivdutt and Queen Kalavati off with the soldiers.

*

The Chunar king and his queen were confined in a house in the city under heavy guard. When Surendra Singh came to meet him, Shivdutt apologized for his misdeeds and promised never to wage war again if the king set him free. Even though he did not trust him, the monarch of Naugarh agreed and even released the Chunar aiyaars Badrinath, Pannalal, Ramnarayan and Chunnilal. All four volunteered to serve Surendra Singh. However, Jeet Singh made them swear an oath of loyalty first.

Then he requested the king to grant him fifteen days' leave—saying Badrinath would officiate in his absence.

'What is it, you've been taking leave off and on—for one or two days at a time,' the king said.

'There were matters I needed to attend to, Maharaj,' Jeet Singh replied. 'But this time I need to go on a journey. You have four competent aiyaars working for you now. Please grant me this favour.'

'All right,' said the king. 'But please return as soon as you can.'

*

The prince and the aiyaars reached the grotto and began to investigate.

'There are signs that someone was here. Maybe they've stolen the treasure too,' Tej said after a while. 'And are holding the princess captive. My teacher told me that there were many magnificent gardens and buildings inside. He even said they were habitable. The marauder might be holed up there.'

'Why are we waiting, then?' said the prince. 'Let's find out!'

Tej made for the source of the stream. He measured forty hands to its north, and began to dig.

'Most likely the key to this mystery, which is written on a metal plate, is buried here,' he said.

But all he found was a letter saying: It is no use digging here now. There is nothing left. The maze has been conquered. Now go and mourn your loss!

'The maze has actually been conquered,' Tej said sadly.

'Well then, all the doors must be open,' Virendra thought aloud.

'Definitely,' Tej replied.

He hurried on, leading them through winding hill tracks. Then he entered a tunnel so narrow that they could walk only in single file. After a while it became wider but was so dark that they had to grope their way. By chance Virendra's hand touched a door. He pushed it open and they found themselves in a garden.

A fountain was playing right in the centre, but they could not find a source for the water. When they neared, they discovered a pair of women's bracelets on the ground.

Virendra picked them up. 'These are Chandrakanta's!' he said, brushing away a tear. 'What are they doing here?'

Tej was about to reply when his eye fell on a piece of paper, folded over like a letter. He picked it up immediately. Be careful, he read, aiyaars will follow you. They should not find out or both you and the prince will suffer a great loss. If I get a chance, I will come tomorrow—to the same place.

Tej frowned. He stood there staring at the letter, confused. Unable to bear the suspense, Virendra asked, 'What's written in the letter?'

In reply Tej just handed it to him. Virendra's eyes widened. 'It sounds as if . . . this is addressed to Bankanya. But who could have written it?'

'It does seem so,' Tej said. 'But there's something even more astonishing.'

'What?'

'The handwriting looks familiar, but I cannot identify it. Someone has deliberately tried to disguise it.'

'Well . . . we'll find out—sooner or later,' Virendra said. 'Let's go on.'

After a while, they found a wall in a corner of the garden, which had four windows opening out in a row. They entered through the one on the left and discovered a door. But they could not go further because there was a steep cliff below. It seemed to be the same door the sage had indicated. They could see the courtyard where Chandrakanta and Chapla had been trapped quite clearly from here.

When they tried the second window they found a wide empty meadow. The sun was too strong, so they decided to go back and try the third window. They entered another garden . . .

'Bankanya!' cried the prince.

She was there, strolling in the garden with some companions! But the moment they set eyes on them, the girls fled to a corner and vanished mysteriously through the walls.

The men chased them till they came to a locked door, which they could not open. Disheartened, they retired to a small pavilion nearby. Virendra slumped on the ground. The aiyaars followed suit.

'How did Bankanya get here?' asked the prince. 'Does she live here? Why did she run away? Doesn't she want to meet me?'

'I wish I could answer your questions,' Tej said, looking gloomily at Devi. The aiyaar shrugged. Even Jagannath shook his head, baffled.

The day passed but they were no wiser. Hungry and tired, they filled their stomachs with the wild fruit growing around and quenched their thirst from a small stream. Finally, they decided to spend the night there.

Devi took out a small lamp from his bag and lit it.

'This is what my love for Chandrakanta has reduced me to,' said the prince despondently. 'And I still have no assurance I will find her.'

'She's safe and sound. You'll definitely be reunited with her,' Tej said. 'And you'll treasure her more, having endured so much anguish to win her.'

'And have you suffered for Chapla's sake?' Virendra's mouth twitched.

'Has *she* suffered for mine?' Tej shrugged. 'It's all for the sake of the princess.'

'Whose daughter is Chapla?' asked the astrologer. 'Would her parents consent to your marriage?'

'Who cares?' Tej said. 'I'll marry her all the same. Or we'll both kill ourselves.'

'If you offer me a reward,' said the prince, 'I'll tell you who her parents were.'

'Okay, I promise you Chapla herself,' Tej smiled.

'Think of it, she'll be mine then,' Virendra raised his brows.

'Yes, yes, she'll be yours, definitely yours,' Tej laughed.

'She too is a kshatriya,' said the prince. 'Her father was a well-to-do landowner. Since her mother died when she was just seven days old, he brought her up and taught her the aiyaar's art. Maharaja Jai Singh regarded him highly and when he died, the king adopted Chapla as a companion for Chandrakanta. You know that the two are like sisters.'

'That's wonderful!' Tej cried, elated. 'I wanted to ask you, but didn't dare.'

This disclosure changed their mood and the night passed in lively conversation. When morning came, they bathed in the stream and returned to the garden.

This time they entered the fourth window and stepped into a lush garden.

'I know this place!' Virendra cried, standing still and looking around. 'This is where I saw Chandrakanta's picture, where I had the meal that made me unconscious. See that tank? I bathed there and . . . just look at those two jamun trees.'

The doors of the rooms were open, so they explored the place freely.

'Here, I sat and ate here,' the prince pointed out.

'The first time you came here,' Devi said, 'you got fine clothes to wear, were served scrumptious fare. No one's offering us anything today.'

'Your exalted presence is responsible,' Virendra teased.

After a while they found a door, which led to another garden.

'This is definitely the same place where I awoke the second time!' Virendra's eyes gleamed. 'Where those women arrested me. But it's completely deserted today. Chitranagar, you're an extraordinary place indeed. How quickly you change! Well, there's another garden left to look at.'

The prince strode ahead and the aiyaars followed him. They were reaching the door that led into the third garden, when a lovely young woman, opulently dressed, appeared. She held out a letter to the prince.

You have been in our neighbourhood for several days, so it is appropriate that we extend our hospitality to you. Please accompany this maiden and bless my humble abode with your presence. I will remember this favour all my life.

Siddhanath Yogi.

The other three read the letter, too. 'It sounds like an order from the holy man,' Tej whispered.

'What should we do?' Virendra said. 'It's growing dark.'

Tej nodded and turned to the woman. 'We are happy to accept the respected sage's invitation,' he said. 'But it's time for our evening worship. We'll come with you after we perform it.'

'I'll wait for you,' the woman said. 'But may I bring some water, prayer mats and whatever else you might need?'

'That's very kind of you,' Tej said.

The woman hurried away.

'If it's the same sage who stopped me from leaping off the

cliff, I'll be happy to meet him,' Virendra said. 'But why did you insist on halting here?'

'I was worried that the venerable sage might trick us,' Tej said. 'Add something to the food to knock us out and dump us outside. All our efforts would be in vain then. Remember what happened to you after you had a meal here?'

'So how do we prevent that?' Devi asked.

'There is one way,' Tej laughed. 'We'll make a paste from the magical flowers and drink it. Then nothing can affect us for seven days.'

'The vaidya who created these flowers must have been extraordinarily clever,' said the prince.

Just then the woman arrived with the requirements for their evening worship.

After they had arranged everything properly, Tej said politely, 'Please, would you leave us for a while? We don't worship in a woman's presence.'

'Why don't you just say that you don't want me around?' The woman stomped off.

After she had gone, they performed their evening puja. Then Tej ground the flower into a paste, which they all drank up.

When the woman returned, they followed her into the other garden. Virendra found it changed—it was not so brightly lit and there were hardly any people. Just a few women strolling here and there, and a minimum of lighting.

The woman escorted them into the courtroom where the picture had been enthroned. But today it was almost empty.

Only the sage, seated on a deerskin, and Bankanya, a short distance from him. Five or six maids stood before them, hands folded. I will not let him get away this time, Virendra vowed. I'll find out who Bankanya is, from where she got the book of mystery and where Chandrakanta is now.

The sage rose. He took the prince's hand and escorted him with great courtesy to a seat near his own. Bankanya stood up and retreated further, gazing at him with lovelorn eyes. Indeed if Siddhanath had not been there, the two would have lost themselves in each other totally.

'You and your companions are well, I hope,' said the sage.

'Thanks to your kindness, but . . . ' the prince paused.

'But what?'

'We are troubled because so much remains hidden from us,' Virendra said. 'But we hope, by your grace all these problems will be solved.'

'By God's grace, all your troubles will come to an end and your doubts forgotten,' Siddhanath announced. 'Please partake of these humble offerings. Then we can spend the night in conversation.'

These words were like nectar to the prince and the aiyaars. Relieved and hopeful, they happily fell on the meal served to them. It was a feast fit for a king. When they had eaten, a beautiful carpet was spread on a stone platform. The sage sat on his deerskin, with the prince next to him. Bankanya sat a short distance away with two companions.

It was a pleasant night. The moon shed a silvery light, and a cool breeze fragrant with the sweet scent of flowers soothed them.

'Now please ask whatever you wish,' the sage said with a smile. 'I'll provide the answers and help you complete all that remains unfinished.'

Many thoughts raced through the prince's mind. What should he start with? Finally he collected himself and began.

'First, please tell me if Chandrakanta is dead or alive?'

'Ram, Ram, who can kill Chandrakanta?' Siddhanath said. 'She's very much alive and well.'

'When can I meet her?'

'Whenever *she* wishes.' The sage pointed to Bankanya.

The prince gazed at Bankanya, who looked anxious and began to tremble. The holy man threw her a stern look and she controlled herself.

'Would you be kind enough to let me meet Chandrakanta?' Virendra turned to Bankanya.

'Don't worry,' the sage said. 'It may be in her hands but she'll do what I say. What else do you wish to know?'

'Who is Bankanya?'

'She's a princess.'

'Why has she done me so many favours?' Virendra asked.

'Because she loves Chandrakanta,' the old man said.

'Then why does she want to marry me?' The prince frowned.

'She doesn't need to, neither does she care for you,' said the sage. 'It's Chandrakanta who insists.'

That pleased the prince. But he said, 'If she's so fond of Chandrakanta, why doesn't she call her here?'

'The time has not come.'

'Why?'

'Only when you fetch Maharaja Surendra Singh and Jai Singh here will she get Chandrakanta, so they can escort her home properly,' Siddhanath said.

'I'll go and get them right away,' Virendra started up.

The sage held up a hand. 'There's something I have to ask you first.'

'What is it?'

'This girl has helped you in many ways. Your aiyaars have seen her. Who else knows about her?'

'No one, apart from Fateh Singh and myself,' the prince replied. 'The aiyaars only set eyes on her today.'

'He has met me once,' Bankanya said, pointing at Tej. 'But I made him promise not to tell you.'

The prince turned to Tej with a puzzled frown.

'This happened the day you said we had forgotten how to practise our art,' Tej replied. 'I tracked her down and said I would pursue her till she revealed herself. She told me not to waste my time. Then I said I'd agree if she promised to make sure that you and Chandrakanta were reunited. In turn, I swore I wouldn't tell anyone that I'd met her.'

'But the men in your camp must have heard that there was an unknown woman helping you,' the sage said.

'No. The aiyaars always discuss these things in private,' the prince reassured him. 'Of course, the men had seen masked horsemen roaming around and delivering letters to me.'

'That doesn't matter,' said the sage. 'But have you

mentioned this to your father or Jai Singh?'

'I only told Jeet Singh,' Virendra said. 'Maybe he mentioned it to my father. But why are you asking? Everyone will praise her for her daring, I'm sure.'

'Jeet Singh would not have told your father,' was the holy man's reply. 'I'm asking because it would upset her parents if they found out that she had been meeting you, writing letters and had even sent you a proposal of marriage. You know this is not considered decent in noble families.'

'But who are her parents?' asked the prince.

'It will all be disclosed when your father and Jai Singh arrive.'

The Mystery Unravels

Since it was already late, Siddhanath insisted that they spend the night there. It was quite warm, so the prince and the aiyaars slept out in the open.

Early next morning, the sage appeared and told Virendra, 'When you fetch their majesties, do not bring them here right away. Leave them at the entrance of the grotto and first come and meet me, along with the aiyaars.'

After a meal, Virendra and the others departed. They reached Naugarh in the evening. Virendra went straight to the palace to meet his parents. But when Tej discovered that his father had taken leave and gone away for fifteen days, he became anxious.

When he asked his mother, the poor woman said, 'Son,

are women in an aiyaar's household considered worthy enough to share their husband's secrets?'

Tej did not know what to say to that. The next day, when Maharaja Surendra Singh asked what they had been doing, he said, 'We went into the cave to search for Princess Chandrakanta and met a holy man there who said, "If you ask Maharaja Surendra Singh and Jai Singh to come here, I'll hand Chandrakanta over to her father." We came back to request you to accompany us there, Maharaj.'

This pleased the king very much and he said, 'Go to Vijaygarh immediately and inform her father.'

*

The garden where the prince had seen Chandrakanta's picture enthroned presented an enchanting scene. The brilliant red rays of the setting sun set the tall trees alight and a cool breeze wafted a sweet fragrance from the flowers. Expanses of fresh green grass were bordered with colourful flowerbeds, while balsam plants stood in rows like multihued troopers standing at attention. Champa flowers bloomed profusely, and a malti creeper draped itself over a frame, covering it with its wealth of blossom. The densely foliaged trees, neatly trimmed hedges and sparkling fountains made it a feast for the eyes.

Three beds had been placed on a marble platform and maids were laying out silken sheets on them.

Three women flitted about the henna bushes, plucking

leaves—Bankanya, who was dressed in white, and two companions in red and green. They turned towards the platform. Suddenly Bankanya dropped her gatherings on the ground and slumped on to the gem-studded bed in the middle.

'I'm tired,' she said.

'Are you tired too?' the one in red asked the other.

'Me and tired?' the green clad one replied. 'After twenty mile rounds in a day?'

'The way we ran around!' The other laughed.

'But the prince's aiyaars never got a clue!'

'Even the astrologer's calculations went awry.' The one in red rubbed her hands.

'The gadgets Siddhanath Baba made us wear rendered his art useless,' Bankanya said. 'The metals they are made of act as a shield.'

'They are definitely very effective,' the girl in red giggled. 'I went disguised as Surajmukhi and the astrologer couldn't find out.'

'The prince must have got fooled too,' Bankanya said.

'Don't ask! He was beside himself,' the girl in red said. 'But we were lucky too. When Shivdutt's aiyaars stole the book of mystery, we discovered them burying it in the forest and dug it out later.'

'How hard it was to persuade Siddhanath Baba to let us roam around,' Bankanya sighed.

'It was for your own good.'

'True, but I longed to see the prince,' Bankanya said.

'He told us to help the prince as much as we could,' the girl in green pointed out. 'Remember how we saved them from Badrinath?'

'What efforts the aiyaars made to find us,' said the other. 'But the Baba is the master of all aiyaars. It was funny when we enticed them to the river bank and stole their clothes!'

'Tej may be clever, but Siddhanath was too much for him,' Bankanya giggled.

'Truly, Siddhanath tricked them well and proper,' the green clad girl said. 'They couldn't even guess that he was helping us to solve the mystery of the cave.'

'I'm sure Tej must have been beside himself when he couldn't open the door of the cave,' the girl in red said. 'He must have thought Surajmukhi was a real devil when she said she'd free Shivdutt.'

'But that scoundrel went back on his promise,' Bankanya said. 'He attacked the prince's men the moment we freed him.'

'We captured him again, didn't we?' said the one in red. 'Krur Singh did recognize us. I knew the game would be up so I did him in. Looks like he was meant to die at my hands.'

'The fool got it into his head that he'd conquer the maze and carry off the treasure,' the green clad girl added.

'I'm ecstatic that I unravelled the maze in the grotto,' Bankanya said.

'It wasn't that hard.' The girl in red shrugged. 'And you had Siddhanath Baba's help.'

'That's true!' Bankanya nodded.

Maharaja Jai Singh left for Naugarh, accompanied by Tej and Badrinath, along with an escort of five hundred men. When he got the news, Surendra Singh went out to welcome him with his nobles and retainers. Virendra and the aiyaars gave Jai Singh a lively account of all the happenings in the mysterious ruins.

The party left for the grotto before daybreak the next day—the two rulers, the prince, the aiyaars and a thousand men. It was not too far, so they reached by sunrise.

When they arrived at the entrance of the cave, Prince Virendra said with folded hands, 'Siddhanath Baba said that if you were agreeable, I should go and meet him alone first.'

'We should go by the sage's advice,' said the two monarchs. 'We'll camp here till you return.'

Accompanied by Tej, Virendra made his way through all the various chambers, houses and gardens to reach the place where he had seen Chandrakanta's portrait. They found Siddhanath Baba standing near the door and greeted him politely.

'We left the others outside, as you suggested,' said the prince. 'With your permission, may we call them in?'

'You are meeting Chandrakanta after a long time,' Siddhanath said. 'Your feelings might overpower you and you might forget that your elders are present and behave inappropriately. It would be better that you two see each other before we call them in.'

These words sent the prince into a paroxysm of delight. How he had been longing to meet his beloved! He had been prepared to give up all, even his life, for her. But how wonderful it was to finally be united with her! The time was appropriate too. There were no worries, no problems to be tackled. All his enemies had been vanquished and nothing lay between them now.

His joy choked his throat, so all he could do was nod and follow the sage on feet that hurried forward on their own. Siddhanath called out to a girl who was plucking flowers, 'Go and tell Princess Chandrakanta that the prince is on his way.'

Tej was equally excited. Lost in their respective thoughts, both followed the sage into the room where Virendra had seen the picture.

At Last!

The prince hurried in and found Chandrakanta standing there with Chapla and Champa, gazing anxiously at the door. He rushed towards her and she towards him. They were so overcome that when just a short distance remained, both fell unconscious! Tej and Chapla were lost in each other too, but they noticed what had happened and hurried to them.

Water was splashed on the lovelorn couple's faces and smelling salts applied to revive them. But even after that, all they could do was sit and gaze at each other and shed tears of joy. Their hearts seemed too full to utter even a single word.

Champa became anxious, thinking they might be losing their sanity. To force them to start talking, she grabbed the princess's hands and said, 'Have you forgotten? You used to say, the day you met the prince you'd ask him who that Bankanya was and what promises he had made to her.'

This jolted the lovers. Till now their gazes had been locked, reading the pain of separation in each other's eyes. The spell broken, they began to chatter so fast that their words sounded like gibberish to the others. However, neither did Chandrakanta complain, nor could the prince ask what she felt about it. They might have really opened up in due course of time if the sage hadn't sent a girl to summon the prince.

'I didn't tell you to spend the whole day with Chandrakanta,' he said. 'Have you forgotten who's waiting outside?'

The prince looked at the sun. It was already afternoon.

'Indeed it is getting late,' he said, embarrassed. 'Shall I fetch them?'

'There is no need to bring everyone. Only those before whom the princess can appear freely,' said the sage. 'And there's no need to tell everyone about meeting the princess.'

It was late by the time the two reached the camp. Therefore Virendra and Tej returned with the two kings and the other aiyaars the next morning.

Both Surendra Singh and Jai Singh were flabbergasted when Tej opened the two locks on the door of the cave. They were even more amazed at the sights inside the grotto. When they came to the last garden, they found Siddhanath waiting at the door to welcome them in.

The kings were about to fall at his feet when he said, 'No one must bow to me, or you won't meet the princess.'

This threw them into a state of confusion. 'Your status is much higher than mine,' the sage said, in explanation.

'But an ascetic is ever worthy of worship,' Surendra Singh said. 'Who are you?'

'Nobody,' said the sage.

'Your words puzzle us greatly,' Jai Singh wrinkled his brow.

'Never mind. Please come into the garden,' Siddhanath said with an enigmatic laugh.

They entered the large hall where the prince had seen Chandrakanta's portrait holding court. Virendra had never seen such lavish decorations before.

Siddhanath first seated them in proper order. After a few words of polite interchange, he said with a smile, 'Now you don't need to search for the princess any longer.'

'We hope that by your favour, we shall meet her at last!' Jai Singh's eyes brimmed with hope.

'You will,' Siddhanath said. 'But please refresh yourself and partake of a meal first.'

When they had finished and were seated comfortably again, Surendra Singh said, 'This charming hill with all these beautiful gardens lies in my kingdom, but no one has ever managed to reach here. Is there any other way out?'

'The path has always been hidden,' Siddhanath said. 'Those who knew about the minor maze might be able to enter. There is another way too, apart from the one you used, but that is even more deeply concealed.'

'How long have you been living here?' Surendra Singh asked.

'I'm here just for a few days,' the sage replied. 'Not for my pleasure, but in the service of my master.'

'Master?' Surendra Singh's brow wrinkled. 'Who is your master?'

'You'll soon find out.'

'His majesty is not aware of this place, you don't live here—so who actually owns it?' Jai Singh asked.

Before Siddhanath could reply, Bankanya appeared. Two companions flanked her, while ten to fifteen maids followed.

The sage pointed to her. 'She owns it,' he said.

The rulers gazed at the girl, astonished. So did the aiyaars. And so did Virendra and Tej. Then the prince recalled all that had happened. He became convinced that Bankanya had imprisoned Chandrakanta and was overcome with rage. This woman is our enemy, he thought.

But when he looked at her again, his anger fled and his love for her prevailed. No, it's not true, he thought. She helped us.

However, this thought sprang up in other minds too.

Maharaja Jai Singh's face grew taut. 'So poor Chandrakanta got trapped here and was imprisoned by this lady?' he burst out.

'No, when Chandrakanta got trapped here, this place did not belong to her,' the sage said. 'She acquired it later.'

These words created further confusion. The prince would have screamed in frustration, but the presence of his elders restrained him.

Then both the rulers turned to the sage and said piteously,

'Please stop talking in riddles and tell us—who is this girl? Who gifted this place to her? And where *is* our dear Chandrakanta?'

Siddhanath smiled and gestured to Bankanya. She stepped forward, along with the two girls dressed in red and green.

The sage pulled off a membrane-like mask from her face, took her hand and presented her to Maharaja Jai Singh. 'Here is your Chandrakanta!'

It was Chandrakanta indeed! She fell at her father's feet. He placed his hands on her head in blessing, then embraced her, overcome with joy.

Siddhanath then removed the masks from the faces of the other two girls. The one in red was revealed to be Chapla and the other in green—Champa!

Surendra Singh thumped Virendra's shoulder, Devi embraced Tej and Jagannath patted both their heads. Everyone smiled and smiled. Jai Singh led the princess to Surendra Singh and asked her to touch his feet.

As for Virendra, his state was beyond description. He squeezed Tej's hand, looked at Chandrakanta with wonderstruck eyes, sighed deeply over and over again.

Siddhanath said, 'You can ask the princess to take the air with her friends while I tell you about this place and narrate the extraordinary story of her adventures.'

'Why can't she stay?' Jai Singh asked. 'I cannot bear to part from her for even a moment.'

'As you please,' said the sage, laughing. 'I knew that this hill contained a small tilism or labyrinth and that there was one in the kingdom of Chunar as well,' he began. 'The one who penetrated it would marry the girl whose dowry this was meant to be. She would acquire it just before the marriage.'

'But please tell me what a tilism is and how it is created,' Surendra Singh asked.

'A tilism is usually created by someone who owns great wealth but is without heirs,' said the sage. 'Such people consult astrologers and soothsayers to foretell if any brave and deserving person is likely to be born in their extended family in the future. The labyrinth is then built and the treasure hidden within it.'

'How can they be sure it'll go to the right person?' Jai Singh asked.

'They rely on astrologers' predictions,' Siddhanath said. 'Great astrologers, soothsayers, tantriks and alchemists are consulted, along with accomplished craftsmen. The course of that person's life is mapped and the treasure is concealed accordingly. The prince will tell you how he conquered the maze.'

'Yes, we will hear the prince's account, but I want to know how my daughter got trapped here,' Jai Singh said. 'And why Shivdutt fled this place, only to be captured again.'

'When the princess got caught in the Chunar labyrinth and arrived at this grotto, she suffered much for two days,' Siddhanath said. 'When I heard, I came here and set her free.'

'But how did you reach her?' asked the prince. 'We came

here too and tried our best, but could not think of a way to get to her.'

'It's not possible to solve a mystery by just thinking about it,' Siddhanath said. 'I knew you were trying to reach her and not succeeding. I could have liberated her then, but I wanted her to win the treasure.'

'But you must have used your yogic powers,' Virendra said.

'I'm not a yogi,' Siddhanath smiled. 'First, I unlocked the door of the grotto. My guru had told me that there were several small gardens in this place. The way to reach them lay through the stream.'

'Oh-h!' exclaimed the prince.

'I entered the stream and after searching for a while noticed a small door in the west. I dived in. After a while, the water receded and I found myself in a tunnel. Within half an hour I reached this garden. I came upon this room and saw that cupboard there. I kicked it and found it was a door that led to a dark enclosure. Then I found another door, which I kicked open too. That led me to the place where I found the princess and Chapla, both in tears. Another path opened into the Chunar tilism, which the prince has conquered.

'I could have taken them home. But I wanted the princess to find the treasure. I also knew that the prince was trying to reach her, not knowing that he too would acquire a treasure on the way. I made the princess and Chapla promise to remain here till this was accomplished—even threatened to abandon them here!

'I really didn't know where the treasure was buried—only that it was meant for the princess. For two days I was preoccupied, trying to find a way to get to it. On the third night, there was a full moon and I was sitting near that tank, lost in thought, when Chapla came running.

' "Please come at once," she cried. "There's something strange here."

'I rose and followed her. Chandrakanta stood by the wall on the east, gazing at something below it. "Look, Babaji," she said. "There's a hole at the base of this wall and large white ants coming out of it! What could be there?"

'My master had told me that the presence of white ants means the key to a treasure was hidden in that spot. I immediately took my dagger from my belt and asked the princess to dig there. She had barely dug a hand's depth when a covered glass jar emerged. I asked her to smash it. A kind of oil flowed out and a bunch of keys was revealed. There were thirty keys in that bunch.

'I asked the princess to go around the garden, looking for locks and try the keys on them. We opened thirty locks with those keys and discovered three doors, which opened out of the ruins from the top of the hill. We also found four other gardens and twenty-three chambers full of treasure and items of luxury.

'When we found the way out from the top, I went home and returned with some maids and essential objects of use for the princess. But she got tired of being confined within this area. So I disguised her and her companions, sent for two or three horses and they were able to roam about outside this warren. Of course, I exhorted them to be careful, so no one could discover their identity. In the meantime, we continued to unearth more riches.

'The prince claimed the other treasure . . . but that's another story.' Siddhanath then turned to Jai Singh and bowed, 'Till now I have regarded Chandrakanta as my daughter as well as my princess. I hand her and her belongings over to you, your majesty . . .

'And as for Shivdutt—the princess took pity on his queen and set them free after he promised to abandon his enmity with the prince. But the villain went back on his word so I captured him and confined him here again. Now . . . if there's anything more you'd like to ask, please do!'

'There's lots I want to ask,' Surendra Singh said, 'But some other time perhaps. All I want to know right now is—why did you help the princess?'

'I have the same question,' Jai Singh said. 'Your statement "I'm not a yogi" baffled me. Who are you? Child, do you know who he is?'

Chandrakanta folded her hands and said, 'I know, but have promised not to reveal it.'

'What's the hurry?' Siddhanath said. 'You'll soon find out. First come and take a look at what Chandrakanta has obtained.'

The sage rose and led them to another garden. He showed them all the gardens, buildings, the treasure and various other goods the princess had acquired.

'Praised be those who amassed this wealth!' Jai Singh cried. 'I could not accumulate one fourth of this, even if I sold my whole kingdom!'

Most of the treasure had been located in the garden and the cellar of the hall where the prince had seen Chandrakanta's picture. After the whole company had explored all the gardens, the chambers and tunnels in the maze, Maharaja Jai Singh again requested the sage to reveal his identity.

'We're eternally in your debt—for rescuing Chandrakanta and helping her in so many ways. But our curiosity cannot be contained now.'

'I will not keep you in suspense any longer,' said Siddhanath with a smile.

He whistled and some maids came running. 'Please set out some water for me to bathe along with the trunk containing my real clothes. Today, I'll say goodbye to my long beard and my deerskin.'

When he reappeared, both Surendra Singh and Jai Singh rushed to embrace him!

'You are more than a brother to me!' said the first. 'A thousand times more!' Jai Singh greeted him as effusively.

As for Tej—when he set eyes on his father, Jeet Singh, his joy knew no bounds. He fell at his feet and Devi followed. Virendra was already basking in the glow of finding Chandrakanta. When he learned he was not obligated to any stranger, but to Jeet Singh, his happiness overflowed.

Jai Singh took Chandrakanta's hand and led her to

Surendra Singh. The princess touched his feet and her father said, 'If you agree, I'll take this girl home and marry her to Virendra in the presence of our relatives and priests.'

'Take her to Vijaygarh immediately,' said the Naugarh ruler. 'Her mother must be pining for her.'

On Jeet Singh's advice, they decided to leave the place and let the treasure remain. It would be recovered later.

A palanquin was sent for to carry the princess, and the monarchs mounted the two horses Chandrakanta and her companions had used.

There was a gate at the south of the garden, with two beautifully crafted iron statues on either side. Jeet Singh went up to the one on the left and placed a finger in its right eye. The figure's belly parted and a silver knob was revealed. He began to turn it, and little by little the gate sank into the ground. A lush green meadow lay beyond it.

'We'll take this path,' Jeet Singh said. Two other figures stood outside and he closed the gate in a similar manner.

The Vijaygarh party went their way and Prince Virendra set off for home. His mother welcomed him with tears of joy. When he had finished telling her all that had happened, he went and paid obeisance to their family goddess.

The Wedding

Preparations for the royal marriage began. The road from Naugarh to Vijaygarh was swept clean and sprinkled with fragrant kewra water. Lamps of crystal were placed on either side.

Prince Virendra's wedding procession set off at an auspicious hour. The arrangements to receive them at Vijaygarh were beyond compare. Fabulously decorated lodgings, sumptuous food and the most accomplished and lovely singing girls to receive them with the most melodious music.

But a strange event occurred when the group arrived. Maharaja Shivdutt was leading the procession, resplendently dressed, a magnificent diamond ornament on his turban, and two swords at his waist. Holding a flag high, he reached the door of the palace where the groom's people were to stay. The party followed him at a leisurely pace.

Prince Virendra arrived, dismounted and was escorted inside with all ceremony. But just as he was entering, a clamour arose on the street.

An extraordinary sight was seen—two Maharaja Shivdutts locked in battle! Their swords flashed furiously. When people tried to intervene, both called out, 'Stay away! There's no need to come to our help!'

One was the Shivdutt who had led the procession. The other was dressed in ordinary clothes but fought bravely. However, the first found an advantage and quickly produced a rope from his waist. He lassoed the other, and dragged him inside. Then he proceeded to tie him to a pillar and taking a torch from a torchbearer, placed it in his hand. After that he went and sat next to Prince Virendra. A golden vessel, studded with jewels and filled with rose water was placed near the prince. Shivdutt dipped a handkerchief in it and wiped his face thoroughly.

The clothes, the ornaments remained the same—only the face that emerged belonged to Tej Singh!

The whole party rolled with laughter. But Tej was simply fulfilling the promise he had made when, during the battle, Devi had brought the spoils of war—Shivdutt's turban ornament, from the enemy camp.

And as for the real Shivdutt, who had vowed to lead an ascetic's life in the forest, he had not been able to overcome his natural villainy. He decided to attend Virendra's wedding to Chandrakanta and search for an opportunity to cause mischief. But when he saw the procession, he realized there was an impersonator mocking him and that stirred up his warrior spirit. He immediately drew his sword to avenge the insult. However, the end result was that he had to play the role of a humble torchbearer while the wedding of Chandrakanta and Virendra was solemnized with great joy and much festivity.

The kingdoms of Naugarh and Vijaygarh were now permanently united. Prince Virendra had already gained Chunar. With the treasure of the tilism added to their coffers, Chandrakanta and he could look forward to a brilliant future.

And of course, Tej and Chapla too soon followed their friends' example!

Translator's Note

Chandrakanta occupies a unique place in the history of the Hindi novel. It was not only a pioneering work of mystery and suspense, but also the first runaway bestseller in the contemporary sense of the word. Perhaps no other Hindi novel has held its readers in thrall over such a long period of time. And while *Chandrakanta* launched a trend for popular fiction, it also contributed greatly to the growth of the Hindi novel and language, particularly the advancement of the Devnagari script.

Like any other author blessed with unprecedented success, Babu Devakinandan Khatri had to fend off many allegations from his detractors. But he was frank enough to maintain that he wrote simply to entertain his readers. He certainly did, because with its incredible flights of fancy, the ingenious twists and turns in the narrative, this book and others that followed were truly 'unputdownable'. No wonder he soon became a cult figure and readers eagerly anticipated his next work.

Chandrakanta was inspired by the author's forays into the jungles of the Chunar region that lies in today's Uttar Pradesh, where he worked as a forest contractor. The mysterious ruins he often encountered and explored had such a powerful effect that he could not help but weave stories around them. Apart from the immediate stimulus of his surroundings, there was a background of literature that influenced his writing. The author himself mentioned the *Kathasaritasagar* as an example of a work that has engrossed readers of a particular era and hoped that his own novels would be similarly remembered. The great Hindi writer Premchand commented that a Persian work titled *Tilism Hoshruba* could also have been a creative spark for Khatri. It was full of devices like knock-out powders, extraordinary disguises and the use of divination that Babu Devakinandan Khatri has consistently employed in his work. However, at its most basic level *Chandrakanta* can be described as the quintessential fairy tale, where the valiant prince has to rescue a beautiful princess from an enchanted place in order to win her hand. The pattern of this traditional narrative scheme is reflected in the obstacles Virendra has to overcome—the machinations of Krur Singh and the ruler of Chunar, trouncing Shivdutt in the battlefield, and finally having to solve the riddles of the tilism to free Chandrakanta.

Translating a classic is a task one cannot help but approach with trepidation. Particularly when your goal is to adapt a work which was the rage in another era, and make it accessible to the young contemporary reader. One has to try and retain the spirit of the original work even while presenting it in a modern-day idiom. Fortunately, a story like *Chandrakanta* is timeless in its appeal, which makes a translator's task considerably easier.

The language of the book is the colloquial Hindustani prevalent at the time—a seamless fusion of Urdu and Hindi. However, much of the usage may not be familiar even to readers of Hindi today. For this reason, providing suitable equivalents in English posed a real challenge. The narrative style is brisk and conversational, and draws the reader into the story, casting such a spell that even the most incredible events seem perfectly believable. But the long passages of dialogue could have proved a stumbling block for young readers. Therefore I decided to condense some of them. Having been written in the form of a serial, the novel cannot help but be episodic; occasionally, I found it necessary to provide transitions to bridge apparently unconnected events. Hence, this rendering of *Chandrakanta* is more of an adaptation rather than a conventional translation.

Coming to the structure, the novel consists of four parts, which are further divided into bayans, or literally narrations. None of these is titled in the original. To provide a more familiar arrangement, I have added chapter headings to the bayans and sometimes combined two or even three to make a cohesive unit, according to the flow of the action. However, since there is no specific separation event-wise where the four parts are concerned, I have not indicated these divisions in the text. For example, the first part ends with the discovery of Chandrakanta and Chapla's bodies and the second begins right in the middle of the same episode. Similarly, the third part commences in the midst of Prince Virendra's discovery of the book of the tilism in Bankanya's hands. This again is probably because of the demands of the serial form. But the course of events does alter in each part. The pace definitely picks up after the first part and the suspense deepens as each new confounding development leaves the reader mystified. The author has so many tricks up his sleeve that the reader remains lost in this labyrinth of story till the stunning dénouement.

While partly dispensing with a sentence-by-sentence translation and tightening the narrative, I have tried to preserve the lyricism of the descriptions and the liveliness of the playful interchange between Virendra, Tej and the other aiyaars. Keeping today's young readers in mind, Virendra's sentimentality had to be tempered to some degree too. The author's asides have been done away with as well. Some portions of the story seemed to require a little detailing to bridge the gap of time that lies between the original book and us. I have also taken the liberty of omitting the bayans in which the intrigues of the two evil aiyaars Zaalim Khan and Aaafat Khan occur, in the fourth part. Though they are typical of the twists and turns the author has employed to enthral the reader, I felt they could be sacrificed without subtracting from the main action. At this stage the plot is in any case moving towards closure.

Translation into English cannot help but dilute the cultural flavour of a book. To retain it as far as possible, some of the original words have been retained and the glossary in the end provides explanations.

Chandrakanta continues to have a dedicated following.

It may be a household name today because of the television serial, which unfortunately took many liberties with the plot. However, it is an exceptional work not just because it is such a masterful tale of mystery and suspense. The element of humour, the relationship between Virendra and Tej and particularly the characters of Chandrakanta, Chapla and Champa—young women who display so much initiative and courage—more than add to its stature as a classic. I sincerely hope I have been able to preserve the spellbinding allure of the original and young people might gain as much pleasure in reading the book as I did translating it.

Finally, I would like to express my gratitude to Prasoon Joshi for kindly agreeing to write the introduction. And a big thanks to my editor Sudeshna Shome Ghosh for her invaluable feedback and meticulous editing.

Deepa Agarwal

Author, poet and translator Deepa Agarwal has written about forty books in English and Hindi, mostly for children. Caravan to Tibet *and* Folktales of Uttarakhand *are two of her recent titles. Apart from several short stories and poems, her translations include a short story collection* Hyena and Other Short Stories *and a novel,* The Crusade, *both originally written by eminent Hindi author Chitra Mudgal.*

Deepa has received many prestigious national awards for her writing, including the NCERT National Award for

Children's Literature for her picture book Ashok's New Friends *in 1992-93.* Caravan to Tibet *was selected for the IBBY (International Board on Books for Young People) Honour List 2008 from India.*

Deepa lives in Delhi with her businessman husband and has three married daughters and two grandchildren.

PUFFIN CLASSICS

Chandrakanta

With Puffin Classics, the story isn't over
when you reach the final page.
Want to discover more about
the author and his world?
Read on . . .

CONTENTS

NAME: Devakinandan Khatri
BORN: 1861, in Muzaffarpur, Bihar, his mother's parental home
CHILDREN: One son, Durgaprasad Khatri, who completed his father's novel *Bhootnath*
DIED: 1913

Where was he educated?

He studied Urdu and Persian during his childhood in Muzaffarpur. Later, when he moved to Varanasi, he learnt Sanskrit and Hindi.

What was his family background?

Devakinandan Khatri's ancestors belonged to Lahore (now in Pakistan). His father, Ishwardas, moved to Varanasi when conditions deteriorated in Lahore after the death of Maharaja Ranjit Singh.

How did he think of writing this book?

Devakinandan Khatri was looking after his ancestral business in Tikari Estate, Gaya, when he found employment with the Raja of Varanasi. The ruler granted him contracts to fell timber in the forests of Chakia and Naugarh. Devakinandan discovered ruined mansions and forts, caves and hillocks hidden away in these dense forests. There was also a place called Jamania near his home, where some mysterious ruins existed. He was very fascinated by these and would often explore them. He came across old tunnels, trapdoors, concealed doors that would suddenly swing open with a touch and other strange devices. He had also heard about the existence of tilisms that were created to guard treasures.

All these experiences stirred his imagination so much that he was inspired to write this tale of suspense and mystery and many other such stories. About the intriguing profession of the aiyaars, the author has written that such people were employed by kings in ancient times to keep their enemies in check without resorting to bloodshed.

What is special about Chandrakanta?

Chandrakanta was a trailblazer—it was the first mystery novel in Hindi and hugely popular. One can well describe it as the Harry Potter of its time. It is said that thousands of people who only knew Urdu, because it was the official language, learned Hindi and the Devnagari script so they could read *Chandrakanta*. The book was published in short chapters or bayans between 1888 and 1891, which were published serially, and people eagerly awaited their release. In fact, groups would gather around one individual who would read it aloud as soon as he got hold of a copy. Critics disapproved and said the novel lacked literary qualities, while the moral police felt the author was corrupting young people but its success continued unabated. Its sequel, *Chandrakanta Santati*, was as great a bestseller. These books were translated into other Indian languages, too. Inspired, many writers began to write mystery novels in a similar vein, though none could equal his achievements. *Chandrakanta* ensured that Devakinandan Khatri acquired a unique place in the annals of Hindi literature for his contribution to the development of the Hindi novel, the growth of the Hindi language and the reading habit. The fact that a TV serial and film have been made based on

the book shows that it still retains a hold on its readers.

Which other books did Devakinandan Khatri write?

Chandrakanta Santati (1894-1905), *Narendramohini* (1893), *Virendra Vir* or *Katora bhar Khoon* (1895), *Kusum Kumari* (1899), *Naulakha Haar* (1899), *Kajar ki Kothari* (1902), *Anuthi Begum* (1905), *Gupta Godana* (1906), *Bhootnath* (1907-1912) are considered his major novels. The last was left incomplete, but his son took up the task and finished it.

What was Devakinandan Khatri like?

He is said to have been a man who believed that life should be lived to its fullest, with a cheerful nature and a generous heart. A professed atheist, he was quite clear about his aims as a writer. He wrote simply to entertain his readers and said that he was following the tradition of the *Kathasaritasagar* and the stories of the *Vetal Pacchisi* (the Vikram-Vetal stories) and the *Singhasan Battissi*, which were leisure reading at one time. Of the extraordinary events that created mystery and added drama to his novels, he said that many of these were based on scientific facts. However, he clearly stated that his stories were not set in any particular period of history. And when his friends suggested he should write on serious matters like religion and patriotism to improve society, he replied frankly that he just wanted his readers to enjoy his books. He felt that by providing gripping books for pleasure reading he had contributed to the spread of the Hindi language, and that was as good a purpose as any. *Chandrakanta*'s success took him by surprise and his readers' responses spurred him on to write more and more.

Kathasaritasagar

The *Kathasaritasagar* was written by Somadeva, a Kashmiri brahmin who composed it some time between AD 1063 to AD 1081 to entertain Queen Suryamati, the wife of King Anantdev. It is derived from earlier works like the *Brihatkatha* of Gunaddhya and is said to be the largest collection of tales, containing twice the number included in the Iliad and the Odyssey.

Many people consider this vast work the foremost example of Indian storytelling tradition. It combines history and myth, reality and fantasy with amazing effect and contains an extraordinary variety of characters and situations. There are stories about actual historical figures along with those about supernatural beings like gandharvas, kinnars and vidyadhars as well as extraordinary female characters. This work also provides amazing insights into human psychology and a vivid glimpse of the social structure, lifestyle, even the geography of the subcontinent.

Vetal Pacchisi

Many individual collections of stories are woven into the *Kathasaritasagar*. The most popular are the King Vikram stories—the *Vetalpanchvishanti* or *Vetal Pacchisi* (Twenty-five Stories of the Vampire) and *Singhasandwatrinshika* or *Singhasan Battisi* (Thirty-two Stories of the Lion Throne). The legendary king Vikramaditya was an actual historical figure, the founder of the Vikrami era which is fifty-six years in advance of the Christian era. He vanquished the Huns and was the ruler of the Malwa region in central India and had his capital in Ujjain.

The vetal, a ghost or vampire, narrates these stories to King Vikramaditya. The framing story says that a mendicant comes to the king's court and asks him to help him in an important ritual. It requires bringing a corpse that hangs from a tree to the burning ground where the ritual was to be performed. When the king picks up the corpse he finds that there is a vetal inside it. While he is carrying it to the burning ground, the vetal tells him a story. At the end he poses a question based on the action of the story, which the king has to answer correctly or die.

Singhasan Battisi

The Singhasan stories are told by thirty-two statuettes to another king, Raja Bhoja who has discovered the throne of King Vikramaditya and is trying to ascend it. The king hears that an ignorant cowherd is transformed into the wisest of judges, even better than the ruler himself, whenever he sits upon a mound on the outskirts of his capital Ujjain and resolves disputes. Surprised, he has the mound excavated. He finds a magnificent throne buried below and prepares to ascend it with great ceremony. But each time he attempts to, he is stopped by one of the thirty-two statuettes at its base, which tell him that only one who is worthy of it can sit on the throne. Then each tells him a story about the king who once occupied it—Vikramaditya. These thirty-two stories do not follow a specific pattern like the Vetal riddle tales but project an exemplary ruler Vikramaditya, who had taken a vow guaranteeing the happiness of his subjects and goes to great lengths to fulfil it. While discharging his duties he has many exciting adventures. The Singhasan stories expound the virtues of valour, ethical action and the duty of the king towards his subjects while providing entertainment through fantasy and suspense. In the *Singhasan Battisi* the vetal is shown to be a powerful vampire in the control of the king who helps him to fulfil his vow.

SOME THINGS TO DO

* We all know about the Himalayas. Find out something about the Vindhya range—where these mountains are located, what kinds of trees and plants grow there and how much of the wildlife mentioned in the book still exists.

* Chunargarh or Chunar is a real place located in eastern Uttar Pradesh. Find out if anything special is produced there and if any important events occurred there.

* Draw a map of the tilism tracing the different routes Chandrakanta, Chapla and Virendra and his party took through it.

* Chandrakanta is depicted as a typical princess who has to be rescued by a prince. Do you think she is actually like that? What is interesting about Chapla and Champa?

* Do you find anything striking about the names of the main characters?

* Virendra is a prince and Tej is his employee. What is notable about their friendship?

* Are there any ruined old houses in your neighbourhood? Have you ever been tempted to explore them? Why?

* What do you think of the aiyaars' tricks and their code of non-violence? Do you think we could defeat our enemies that way?

★   Is the tilism actually a magical place?

★   Have you read any other popular novels written in your mother tongue?

(in order of appearance)

Prince Virendra Singh: the son of Maharaja Surendra Singh of Naugarh, in love with Chandrakanta

Tej Singh: the son of Jeet Singh, the prime minister of Naugarh, an accomplished aiyaar

Krur Singh: the son of Kupath Singh, the prime minister of Vijaygarh, who plans to marry Chandrakanta and occupy her father's throne

Nazim and Ahmad: aiyaars employed by Maharaja Jai Singh of Vijaygarh, who are on Krur's side

Chandrakanta: the beautiful princess of Vijaygarh, who is in love with Virendra Singh

Chapla: her lively companion, who is an accomplished aiyaara

Champa: Chandrakanta's companion, who is learning the art of aiyaari from Chapla

Maharaja Surendra Singh: Virendra's father, the ruler of Naugarh

Devi Singh: Tej's disciple, who is learning the art of aiyaari from Tej

Maharaja Jai Singh: Chandrakanta's father, the ruler of Vijaygarh

Maharani Ratnagarbha: Chandrakanta's mother, the queen of Vijaygarh

Maharaja Shivdutt: the ruler of Chunargarh

Pandit Jagannath: astrologer and aiyaar at Shivdutt's court

Badrinath, Pannalal, Ramnarayan, Bhagwandutt, Chunnilal and Ghasita Singh: aiyaars employed by Shivdutt

Hardayal Singh: prime minister of Vijaygarh, employed after Krur's disgrace

Jeet Singh: prime minister of Naugarh and Tej's father

Maharani Kalavati: Shivdutt's wife, queen of Chunar

Fateh Singh: the commander-in-chief of the Naugarh-Vijaygarh army

Bankanya: a mysterious maiden who appears in the forest and claims to be in love with Virendra

Surajmukhi: an ugly hag who threatens to create problems for Virendra if he does not marry her

Baba Siddhanath: an old ascetic who helps Virendra to find Chandrakanta

GLOSSARY

aiyaar: a person adept in various arts like disguise, trickery, espionage, the knowledge of herbs, the use of arms, music and dance, employed by rulers in earlier times

aiyaara: a female aiyaar

apsara: celestial dancer at the court of Lord Indra

asharfi: gold coin formerly in use worth between sixteen and twenty-five rupees

Babaji: respectful term of address for an elderly person

baithak: sitting room

been: snake charmer's flute, made from a gourd

bel: wood apple, offered to Shiva in worship

bela: jasmine flower, *Jasminum zambac*

ber: small plum-like fruit

bhairavi: in Hindustani classical music a melody sung or played in the early hours of the morning

Bhootani: demoness

chiraunji: the tree *Buchanania latifolia* and its nut

Chitranagar: literally, city of the picture

chormahal: secret apartment, meant for women

Dakini: a demoness; witch

dewan: prime minister

dharma: customary code of religious and social conduct

dhoti: a piece of cloth worn around the lower part of the body

durbari: here, the name of a melodic composition in Hindustani classical music

guruji: respected teacher

Hai: expression of lament

huzoor: mode of address used for a person of high standing

Jai Maya: 'Hail illusion', the aiyaars' greeting

jamun: the rose apple tree, *Eugenia jambolana*, or *Syzygium jambolanum* and its fruit

juhi: a kind of jasmine, *Jasminum auriculatum*

kewra: the screwpine, *Pandanus odoratissimus* and its fragrant flower

khanjari: a small tambourine; musical tongs with discs used by sadhus

kroom-dhoom-fateh: a particular drum beat signifying victory

kshatriya: a member of the warrior caste

loo: the hot wind that blows in May and June in the north Indian plains

Maharaj: form of address for a person of high standing

malti: a kind of jasmine

motia: a kind of jasmine

neem: the margosa tree, *Melia azadirachta*, known for its antiseptic and medicinal properties

oruhar: a kind of flower

paan: betel leaf

peepul: holy fig tree, *Ficus religiosa*

Pitaji: respected father

Ram, Ram: invoking the name of Ram, here an expression of concern

sadhu: a holy man; an ascetic

sakhu: the teak tree

Sartod Singh: head breaker, spoken in defiance here

Surajmukhi: sun-faced, beautiful, here used mockingly; sunflower

tantriks: practitioners of tantra, a body of spells for the attainment of magical powers

tika: an ornament for the forehead

tilak: mark made on the forehead; here, a sign of investiture

tilism: the work or creation of magic

vaidya: an ayurvedic doctor
Viyogini: a woman separated from her lover or husband
wah: an expression of appreciation
yogi: a practitioner of yoga
yogini: female practitioner of yoga